Buck Fifty

a novel by

Saga

KingPen Ink

Buck Fifty

ISBN-13: 978-0-9753966-2-9

Published by KingPen Ink
First Printing Jan 2008

Address all inquiries to:
King Pen Ink
P.O. Box 6411
Bridgeport, Connecticut 06606

www.TheKingPen.com

Printed in the United States of America.

This book is dedicated to
you.

Time is money,
so I sincerely thank you
for spending it
with me.

Shouts

First and foremost I give thanks to the All, for She has led the way and has been oh so merciful. He has blessed me with the experience necessary for wisdom and overstanding, though the more I learn the less I know.

To my moms D.S I love you. Not only nine months, you held it down for 33 years.

To my SUN A, you are so bright to be so young. Daddy loves you forever and a day, plus an extra hour. Keep shining little me.

To C.T, Love is the law, Love under will. Muah! Can we live?

As I pour my stout over imaginary graves I say Ashë to all my family and friends who were upgraded over the years. A special Rest In Peace goes to auntie P and uncle L and Danielle Stevens. To my blood still on earth and everybody else who got love for your boy lets live as if today is our last!

To all those full time haters who pray and pray for my downfall just imagine my middle finger held high and to all you bitch ass distributors and publishers, my new name is AKA smack your favorite author. Playin wit my bread is like playin wit ya life.

All my Bridgeport massive lick a shot in the air! You can't tell us nothin! Bloody stand up! Every side of town stand the fuck up!

To every shorty in every project that copped my book or borrowed it I got love for you baby. For all my niggas locked down stressed the fuck out stay focused you'll be home soon. One!

To all my fellow authors who speak and keep it humble. You know what it iz.

To all my street merchants in the five boroughs moving my books like 022's, keep makin'um believe it. PEACE to every distributor that pays on time and to every independent bookstore across the globe that sells my books. One love! Catch me in the hood!

Saga

Buck Fifty

a novel by

Saga

KingPen Ink

Bloody Prelude

Slowly she emerged from the clear blue sea onto the hot white sand. The sun's blazing glare surrounded her face and her body glimmered like a 15-carat diamond as the water dripped from each succulent curve. I glanced with envy finding myself totally entrenched. My eyes gazed upon her radiant black skin with jealousy, as pure resentment rushed through my veins like a hot dose of heroin. Plastic surgery could never bestow a figure like that. This girl was a natural.

Soon her stride seemed to glide toward me as if her feet were on casters. The sunshine vanished and the sky became violent with gloomy clouds and roaring thunder. In that instant I recognized Kayla's ferocious stare. In a panic attempt to grab the gun from under my beach chair I froze and it was too late.

"Payback's a BITCH!" Kayla uttered, then "*WWWOOOSSSHHH,*" her blade made a slicing sound through the wind before it slashed my throat.

The bleeding wouldn't stop and my head started spinning in delirium. My whole life played out before me in what felt like seconds. I couldn't believe I was going out like this. My eyes closed shut then everything faded as I fell sideways in the sand.

Even though I was only dreaming, I awoke as if my nightmare was a reality. The bed sheets were soaked with sweat and the warm menstrual blood in the center caused me to panic even more.

"No! Stop! Nooooo!" I screamed, as I jumped out of bed swinging my arms in a wild rage.

"Honey it's all right, it's okay. It was just another bad dream," my husband reassured, while he struggled to snap me out of it, "just relax and take deep breaths," he said as he coached me back to sanity.

This disturbing revelation of being murdered at the hands of someone I betrayed had been haunting me every night for two weeks straight now. Between all the rotten bastards I killed and fickle girlfriends I backstabbed, it was a miracle that I even lived this long. Here I was supposed to be enjoying my new life without looking back, but I couldn't stop thinking about Kayla. Out of all of them I knew she would be the one to track me down and settle the score, because of what I did to her. They say we all have to pay for the things we do in life and lately I've been feeling like my time to finally pay was near.

With all the wild shit floating around in my head I couldn't go back to sleep no matter how hard I tried. So while my husband checked his messages, I ran a hot bubble bath before rolling up a nice fat blunt to calm my nerves. If we were home at our beach house

I would have swam butt naked in the ocean like I always do, but since we were on vacation I soaked in the hotel's spacious jet tub to relax.

As the potent island weed took affect, I placed cucumber slices on my eyelids and let my mind wander. Drama filled memories played out as the bubbles gradually dissolved into the water. My thoughts drifted all the way back to high school, which was the point where it all began...

Buck Fifty

My First

I was always told that it ain't where you're from its where you're at, and where I was I did not want to be. See I wasn't always a sex-addicted cokehead with a big ole juicy behind and humongous breasts. On the contrary I was just a prissy flat butt chick from the suburbs, bored out of my fucking mind. The place to be was in the hood so I thought, because that's where all the excitement seemed to be going down.

Hardhead was my middle name. Whatever my father told me not to do I did. He used to try to tell me who I could and could not talk to, but I wasn't having it. I did things my way or no way at all. By the time I entered the ninth grade, I made up my mind to fulfill a burning desire I had smoldering between my thighs. In all honesty I can't stand those motherfuckers now, but back in the day... let me tell you. I would have done just about anything to get my mouth around some long hard chocolate.

On a warm spring day after soccer practice there he was, my first official piece of dark meat. James was his name and he worked as one of the school's groundskeepers. I had my eye on him for a minute now and whenever I seen James with his shirt off a mushroom cloud of lust would detonate in my crotch. By the way James carried himself I could tell that he was imported from the city. James had a bounce in his step and he often wore a oversized fitted Yankee cap tilted forty-five degrees to the left with a doo-rag underneath to cover his lustrous waves. I also loved the way James's gold chains sat between his curved-in pectoral muscles and how he let his *Dickies* sag below his boxers.

James had a swagger that was new to me and although the man was more than twice my age, I didn't feel like I was sweating an old man. His youthful smile and stylish manner made him appear much younger than he actually was. Anyway like any other landscaper, James cut the grass and took care of the surrounding fields where our high school soccer team practiced. He had no idea that I had a better job in store for his fine black ass.

During each practice I would run up and down the grassy turf in my sexy uniform skirt and sometimes it would blow up revealing my thong underwear, if I wore any at all. One day James shot a glance my way as he rode alongside the fence on his lawn mower dripping with sweat. I figured a little exhibitionism would turn him on. I looked back as I bent over and slowly licked my lips when we made eye contact. James smiled like I was silly then quickly turned left on his John Deere. A short distance away from the school was a puny supply shack that stored weed-whackers and other landscape equipment, so while the rest of the team hit the showers after practice I drifted down the hill to pay James a friendly visit.

To my advantage I strolled in on him smoking a joint, while the faint sound of Dancehall music played in the background. James had his size thirteen boots plopped up on a tool-infested desk. He appeared to be enjoying himself, but he was too busy getting high to notice me blocking the entrance. I just watched for a second as he blew smoke through his nostrils before clearing my throat to make my presence known.

"See if I was the police you would've been busted," I said with a flirty smile.

"Can I help you?" James coughed, as he brushed ash from his sweaty wife beater.

"We're finally alone" I spoke softly as I walked up to him, "I see the way you look at me and I can tell that you want some of this."

"Some of what?" James questioned oddly with his eyes red as hell.

"Some of this!" I answered, while massaging my nipples in his face, "act like you know."

To add to James' surprise I quickly unsnapped my skirt then lowered my white lace panties with both thumbs. My electric razor trimmed bush was now exposed, but James backed away as if my pussy stank to high heaven.

"Yo I don't know what you think you're doin' but you betta' stop it before I__"

"Before you what tell on me!" I raised my tone as I plopped down in his lap, "What are you going to say" I kindly picked pieces of grass from his collar, "that you were smoking weed with one of the underage students whose father has donated tons of money to this school?"

Next I snatched the joint from the ashtray and hit the weed like I've been smoking for years. After blowing rings of smoke in his face I locked eyes with James again and then slowly passed my hand over his gorgeous chest.

"Listen baby if you want to keep this bullshit nine to five I suggest you give me what I want or I'm telling the principal. You know how much Mr. Kravitz hates black people."

James looked at me like I was crazy then pushed me out of the way. Brushing me aside only riled my temper, so I ran to the exit screaming like I was really in trouble. It was all a put on, because I knew no one in the school could hear me all the way from the supply shack, but James didn't know if I was serious or not. As he aggressively pulled me back inside the door he covered my mouth with his large coarse hands.

James didn't know that I liked playing ruff and the more he took control, the more I became aroused. My hole began to heat up like grease in a frying pan and I could even feel my clitoris tingle in anticipation of finally getting what my father dreaded.

"Are you fuckin' crazy?" James shouted, while he shook the hell out of me, "let's go I'll take you to the office myself."

As I cried uncontrollably in the corner, threatening to go to the police instead, James stopped rebuking me. His voice faltered then he held his head in his hands.

"If I lose another job" he thought out loud, "my P.O is gonna' violate me for sure... I'm not goin' back to jail over some horny lil' white bitch fuck that!"

"Who said you have to go to jail or lose your job" I interjected, while wiping my crocodile tears away "if you whip it out for me I won't tell nobody anything. I promise I'll be a good little girl," my eyes twinkled with sexual hunger.

"Why you gotta' fuck wit' me?" James asked as he continued to fret, " why me?"

I wanted to say 'cause I heard you got a big ass dick!' but I didn't.

Since James was on parole at the time, he needed his $8 dollar an hour job to stay out of prison and feed his family. I had James right where I wanted. He knew that if I accused him of fondling me people would believe my story, rather than take the word of a two-time felon with marijuana in his system.

Either way James knew he would get fired, so without any enthusiasm he unzipped his blue work uniform slacks. James facial expression was just as lifeless as his dangling penis. It was obvious that he didn't want to fuck me as much as I thought he did, so I dropped to my knees to give the man some incentive. I licked the length of his floppy dick until it began to swell. In no time a ramrod filled my mouth as I jerked and pulled. I could barely get my hands around his fat trouser snake, so I used both hands and sucked it some more until my jaw became sore.

Since James was so well endowed, I was afraid that his thick dick was going to hurt more than pleasure me. Therefore I carefully backed onto his meat pole like a truck driver cautiously backing into a loading dock. Aching bliss was the only pain to be felt. My sopping wet vagina slid tightly around his cock as I whimpered with delight.

"Oh yeah that's it drive it in all the way," I carried

on pushing back with each stroke.

In the manner in which I rotated my hips James could no longer pretend to be uninterested. The punany had the nigga talking.

"Damn it's so hot and tight," he moaned in shock before bending me over a chair.

I knew it felt good, because he put his back into it like every man should. With my eyes closed I bit down on my lip as he started to pump harder and faster. The sound of James's balls slapping against my ass sped up as he proceeded to rabbit fuck me. The faster he plowed the more I screamed with joy.

"Oh my god! Give it to me daddy! Plunge that dick harder! Yes! Yes!" I howled in ecstasy, "give it to me, I'm 'bout to cum!"

Seconds later I came or better yet, I arrived! Before James could bust off inside me, I kneeled before him like he was a priest and I was a parishioner receiving communion. My tongue was out at full length and with one eye shut I prepared for a hot sperm blast. When I stood up to swap fluids with James, he pulled my hair back like he was going to kiss me at first. But instead he hog spit down my throat before shoving my face to the floor.

"You got it twisted," James sneered, "I don't kiss filthy Babylon hoes! Now get the fuck outta' here before I decide to catch a case!"

I felt too relieved to get mad at that point, because I got what I wanted. The blood in my veins pulsated. I was thoroughly energized and James' disrespect kind of turned me on. While James re-looped his belt I wiped off the DNA from my chin then snapped my skirt back on before leaving.

"Were you this easy to fuck when you were locked up?" I taunted walking away.

"Take you and your flat ass up the hill before I slap you with this rake! You got what'chu wanted now get!"

Apart from James' comment about my ass, I still felt powerful as ever. In the same way as my ancestors used their slaves for sex, I too had conquered a black man caught in the system. Although I never fucked James again after our little episode, I bet he still thinks about the 14-year-old white girl who pimped him like one of Willie Lynch's daughters.

Kayla

The next day while I sat Indian style on my bedroom floor a classmate braided my hair. The phone rang, but I could barely hear it over the Mary J album we blasted.

"Quick hand me the phone before my father picks it up," I hollered over the backdrop of *I can love you better,* "it's probably one of my niggas checking up on me."

"I don't work here," Kayla retorted with a haughty attitude, "and don't be using the N word around me like that either bitch!" Kayla sneered, as she pulled my braid tighter and tighter.

As soon as I picked up the phone I knew exactly who it was.

"*This is a collect call from the Webster Correctional facility from- [MANNY],*" the automated operator instructed, before Manny's actual voice interrupted, *"to accept this call say yes after the tone."*

"HELL-NO!" I screamed into the receiver before slamming the phone down, "that boy Manny's a pain in the ass!" I sighed right afterward.

I had plenty of dudes calling me on the regular, but not that many from prison. It seemed like Manny wasn't even locked up, seeing how frequently he called. From the one time I talked dirty to Manny, while he jerked off over the phone he hadn't stopped calling me collect since.

"What's he doing calling you anyway?" Kayla interrogated before finishing the last line of cornrows, "my girl got a baby by Manny...let me find out you messin' 'round wit' her man?"

"Yuk! What could, *can you please send me a money order,* begging ass Manny do for me? Not a damn thing! I don't want his ugly ass," I responded defensively, "That bitch could have 'em!"

I could admit now that I was the type of chick to make you think your man was ugly then fuck their brains out the first chance I got, but in Manny's case he was really ugly and I could truly care less about that dude.

"Trust me Kayla he's the last thing on my mind," I frowned, then smiled devilishly "I got my freak on with a real man yesterday."

"You are such a liar Jaz," Kayla rolled her eyes, "I was with you all day yesterday."

"Not after practice you weren't! Remember that cute guy with the Yankee cap that cuts the grass and shit? The one who I said looks at me like he wants to blow my back out?"

"Yeah I know who you talkin' bout," Kayla shrieked with skepticism and excitement, "he tried to talk to me the other day while I was waiting for the bus."

"Well" I said, after wetting my lips, "your girl put it on that nigga like the Queen bee," I admitted before humping the bed to demonstrate how I worked it.

As Kayla stared at me to see if I was lying I examined my hair in the mirror as I sang along with Lil' Kim.

"*Dippin on ya Ninja Honda wit Tanisha and Rhonda... what!*"

Using the N word and sharing the juicy details with Kayla seemed to offend her a little, but fuck Kayla. To me she was a crumb from the ghetto that I was using like everyone else. Who was she to tell me what words I could use.

"*Jasmine is that a cigarette I smell?*" My father hollered from the hallway, "*and who was that on the phone?*" He asked, now standing outside of my door.

"Nobody dad, wrong number," I lied.

"*Is something burning in there*?" My father queried, as he tried to open my bedroom door.

"No! God! I was just burning incense," I replied sourly with my foot blocking the door so he couldn't get in, "can we get dressed in private please!"

"*Well you're going to be late for the game if you don't hurry up.*"

"Aw'right already, we'll be down in a minute," I chuckled behind the door while dying out my cig.

After tossing the empty beer bottles and blunt contents under my bed, we ran down the stairs and hopped in the car.

My father tried to be strict, but I was out of his control. He disliked black people for the most part, but for unknown reasons he didn't mind me hanging out with Kayla. Although daddy was a closet racist, his favorite athletes and musicians were all black. He knew every player in the NBA by name and could tell you their career stats off the top of his head. I'm not even going to go into his fascination with Venus and Serena Williams. When I asked him *how come you always watch sports dominated by a race of people you hate?* My father's answer was o*h black athletes aren't like regular blacks.*

Anyway Kayla happened to be the star athlete at my school, but I don't think that was the reason why he liked her so much if you know what I mean.

"How's my favorite goalie?" Daddy asked as soon as we got in the car, "why don't you sit up front with me Kayla? We can talk about last week's scrimmage."

"No that's okay Mr. O'Reilly I'm fine back here with Jaz," Kayla said, as she made a face at me like my father was bugging.

Kayla's perception was right on point. My father was really acting weird. He kept fixing his crotch and adjusting the rear view mirror to get a better look into the backseat. It seemed like he was trying to steal a look at Kayla's shiny sexy legs. He kept smiling oddly and I even think that my father had a hard-on. The look in his eye was familiar to me because it was the same look I displayed when I seen something I wanted to explore.

Kayla wasn't from the wealthy suburbs of Fairfield, Connecticut like myself. She was from the poor inner city of grimy ass Bridgeport, the largest garbage dump in the state. The only reason Kayla and I attended the same school was due to a publicized accusation that Laurelton Prep, a selective private school for girls of a certain social class, was running a racist establishment.

Laurelton Prep's black student enrollment was at a whopping 2%. Minority leaders exposed this fact, which compelled the $1200 a month institution to set up some kind of integration system. To remedy all the bad publicity, the school bussed in a few token black students from surrounding areas to make the politicians happy. Based on her outstanding athletic ability and her family's qualifying low income, Kayla made the list.

Far removed from my priorities, boys or should I say dick, was second in Kayla's book. Maintaining a decent grade point average so she could get into college was numero uno on her list. Although I was the one who was chauffeured to school in a Benz and lived in a big fancy house with expensive clothes in my closet and had everything a girl could ask for, I still envied Kayla for some reason.

Kayla and I were both 14, but she had a grown woman's shape and sense of pride that I did not. She was petite from the waist up, but from the waist down the girl had that thunder down under. Kayla's apple bottom was way beyond rotund. It resembled two halves of a basketball attached to her lower back and seeing the way guys looked at her made me jealous to no end, because my butt was flat and somewhat boyish.

With those track star thighs of hers and hand size breasts that curved upward, Kayla was definitely stupefying. The small birthmark under her left eye only enhanced her otherwise impeccable dark chocolate complexion. No one could doubt Kayla's physical beauty and standing next to her made me look like a pale pancake with legs. It was hard to deal with all the people goofing on how horizontal my butt was compared to hers, but I'll explain how I changed all that later.

Over time Kayla and I became sort of close. Although I must admit that I bought her friendship by paying good money to have my hair braided every week. To get out the house on the weekends I would even give Kayla a little extra cash if she would let me hang out with her in Bridgeport. Whenever Kayla and I hung out together dudes would always speak to her first and I hated that shit. It was sickening how many sexy ballers she shot down, whereas I was not even approached once.

Since Kayla always seemed uninterested I would slip the cute ones my number on the low, but they never called. Probably because they thought I was desperate. Who knows? Even though I often felt unattractive when I was with Kayla, I still felt like rolling with her was a good way to explore the city streets my father kept me away from all these years. Kayla didn't know it, but she was going to be my personal ghetto tour guide.

When there was a party or a club I just had to go to I would sometimes borrow my father's Benz without his permission. I made sure my face was seen cruising every ruff block in the city and I always hit the projects to make a good impression on the hustlers.

Eventually I got Kayla to loosen up on her 'books before boys' policy. I even swayed Kayla to smoke a little weed once when we double dated the hottest thugs in the hood. As soon as the word got out that there was a frisky white girl in the hood eager to give up the booty my popularity increased 100%. Kayla thought I was stupid for giving it up so easy, but I think she was just jealous now that I was the center of attention and she wasn't.

When the time came for us to prepare for finals,

I convinced Kayla to let us study at her crib instead of staying at the dreadful library. After we got off the bus we cut through the Greens housing project as a short cut to get to her house. I was fascinated. It was as if I was watching a real life rap video. There were crowds assembled in front of each brick building with fancy cars pulling into the lots nonstop. The usual suspects hopped in and out of vehicles conducting business I assume, because they all were counting money. As we walked passed building 5 one of them asked me if I was straight, but I didn't know how to respond.

"Yeah we're straight" Kayla responded, while she grabbed my arm and walked me away.

"What did he mean *are you straight*?" I questioned Kayla.

"Are you a crack head?" Kayla posed.

"Hell no!" I answered.

"Then trust me you're straight, so let's go!"

"Hold up Kayla how 'bout we study later and see what's going on out here instead? I always wanted to date a drug dealer."

"Ain't shit going on around here except trouble. You could stay here if you want, but I'm going home."

All I could do was suck my teeth. If I had known that we were going to actually study, I would have paid some other chick to braid my hair and hang out with her instead. I wanted to parlay in the projects for a while and check out the drug scene, but Kayla was acting like a real buster.

When we finally got to Kayla's building I was surprised. It was unlike I expected. The first floor apartment was small of course, but it was nice and clean for the most part and there was beautiful African statues and art all over the walls. I didn't see one roach or rat. My father used to always say that niggers were nothing more than lazy porch monkeys living off of taxpayer's money, but Kayla certainly made it clear that statistically there were more white people collecting welfare than blacks.

"You look so surprised," Kayla said, noticing my shocked reaction, "just because a person has limited funds does not mean they have to be dirty."

It was obvious that Kayla's parents were decent hard working people. They were nothing like the ones portrayed on cable or television.

"Damn Kay, why'd we have to leave though? I wanted to see some real hood action," I griped, as I threw my book bag on the couch, "you know... like a drive-by or a drug deal gone bad or something gangsta like that."

"Okay... how 'bout I punch you in the face then sell you some Advil for the headache afterward... is that gangsta enough for your dumb ass?" Kayla smirked before she cracked open her science textbook.

My Bad

After two long hours of cramming for finals, we took a break to watch BET.

"Before we start studying again can I at least smoke some of this weed I got first? I been wanting to test this shit all day."

"Go ahead knock yourself out," Kayla answered, "just blow it out the window and make sure you lock it after you're finished cause my father don't like my friends hanging out of his window talking to strangers. He thinks it's uncouth."

Thirty minutes later Kayla curled up in her parent's nice warm bed where she fell asleep. I guess she was tired from practice and studying, so to pass the time until my ride showed up, I kicked it with the scores of people that passed by Kayla's window even though she said not to. It was fun acting like I lived there. I met a few cuties and got a couple of numbers before this creepy looking dude started bothering me.

"Excuse me lady... you um... you got five dolla's I could borrow? I ah wanna' get something to eat," he asked as he peeked over my shoulder into the living room.

I felt sorry for the man, so I dug into my pocket and donated a twenty after he ran down a story about running out of gas and being late for work.

"Ooooh that's a nice stereo system," he looked over my shoulder than fixed his eyes back on me, "ya mind if I hit some of that?" The man asked, as I fought with my lighter to burn the weed.

Dude started to really freak me out cause he kept scratching his arms and rocking back and forth as he watched the blunt intently. He looked crazy and when I noticed all the sores on his arms I regretted sharing my blunt with him. I thought to myself that he must be high on something else already and just wanted him to leave.

"Here you go you can have the rest of this cause my boyfriend will be here soon and he wouldn't appreciate me talking to you understand?"

Weirdo mumbled something slick under his breath than left. I didn't hear a thank you or nothing for the money and weed I donated. Before I leaned back into the apartment I noticed my father's Mercedes coming down the block ten minutes earlier than expected. I left without saying bye to Kayla cause she was still knocked out and I didn't want to wake her.

Hours later, while I was home on the phone with one of my new male friends, Kayla's father was just getting off of work. Just as any other night he made his way down Harral Avenue, when all of a sudden he noticed something strange. The living room window was left wide open and the drapes were blowing outside in the wind with a garbage can stacked underneath the ledge.

Being the fortified Vietnam vet that he was, Kayla's father became alarmed since crack heads and dope addicts were notorious for creeping through first floor windows. He jumped out the car and crept up the staircase at the same time reaching for his pistol. Kayla's father always felt that living on the first floor without security bars attached to the windows was dangerous, but Kayla's mother was against the idea. She didn't want her family to feel like prisoners in their own home.

Just as Kayla's father put the key to the lock he heard a panicky clatter. He pushed his way into the apartment with his gun drawn, quickly firing three shots at the tall and thin shadowy figure scrambling through the living room.

"Pop! Pop! Pop!" The .380 fired.

Both Kayla and her mother screamed as the gunshots frightened them out of bed. When Kayla's father burst into the bedroom, there lay his wife bleeding on the floor holding her stomach. Kayla's father blanked out like he was back in Vietnam again. The weirdo I gave twenty dollars to was dead. Kayla was hysterical, because she couldn't comprehend what was going on or why her mother was dying on the floor.

When Kayla's father had fired his weapon, he hit the drug-induced burglar with all three shots. However in spite of the mans' accuracy, the last shot went right through the crack head's skinny body piercing the bedroom door before fatally striking his wife as she jumped out of bed. It was my bad cause if I had locked the window like Kayla instructed me to do none of this would have happened. I should've listened.

Some would say the court system in Connecticut was fucked up. I would agree. Kayla's father was improperly sentenced to ten years in prison, for involuntary manslaughter and aggravated assault on top of a list of weapons charges when police found other guns in the house.

For obvious reasons Kayla never returned to Laurelton Prep after that night. It was truly a tragic case of events. I know how she must have felt about losing her mother, because I lost my mother at an early age as well. I really cried for Kayla, true story, but I probably cried more for myself because my ghetto pass had expired and I was fresh out of black girlfriends.

Soon after Kayla watched her pops get taken away in shackles, she was sent to Brooklyn, New York to live with an aunt in the Van-Dyke housing projects. I knew Kayla's father was not too fond of his daughter being raised in the perilous projects after all the trouble he and his wife went through to keep their daughter out of trouble, but he could do.

As time went by I became more familiar with the hood on my own. I learned what was hot and what was not from watching rap videos and reading hip hop magazines. Material wise I had the around the way look down pat, but when I think about how silly I must have looked rocking blonde cornrows and big gold earrings with my name in the middle all I can do is laugh. I bit Kayla's whole style from the slang that she used, down to the ditty in her bop. However nothing I did made me desirable like her. I was still missing something.

One day while I sat on my bed skimming through

an old Nike shoebox full of letters and pictures, I came across some Polaroids Kayla and I had posed for in a nightclub. In this one particular pic I was sitting in a large wicker chair behind a graffiti backdrop, while Kayla and her friend Nikki popped out their hips and stuck out their chest.

That's when it hit me. The curvaceous shapes Kayla's body flaunted in the photo gave me the dazzling idea to get cosmetic surgery. Thick was the way to be and the only things thick on my body were my eyebrows. When I mentioned the idea of a cosmetic makeover to my father he flipped.

"What's the big deal? Jenny got a boob job before she went off to college," I pled my case.

"Your sister was eighteen at the time and you young lady still live at home under my roof. I don't want to hear it. No."

For hours I daydreamed about all the attention I could get and how men would fall to my feet in admiration of my new enhancements. But first I had to somehow convince my father that it was essential to my mental health that I get breast implants, so I called my older sister in California for some quick advice. She explained to my father over the phone that it was common for girls my age to get nose jobs and tummy tucks or whatever kind of cosmetic surgery they needed to improve their self-confidence.

"Dad a girl needs to feel good about herself," Jenny said with know how, "implants are the new makeup get with it daddy. You wouldn't want your daughter to grow up feeling inadequate now would you?"

My father was not going for Jenny's confidence skit. He made up his mind and that was it. No matter how much I begged for the money his response was dead set against it.

"I'm not paying any lousy doctor to make my daughter look like a teenage porn star. When she turns eighteen and moves out on her own she can do whatever she wants to do to her body like you did Jennifer, but until then the answer is absolutely not!"

I didn't give a shit what my father said. I never listened to him before, so why would I start listening to him now. I made up my mind that I was getting plastic surgery no matter what I had to do to get the money. Even if that meant doing something that could land me in prison.

We Fly High

My summers off from school were always spent on the west coast of California. Usually I despised packing my bags to go spend my vacation with phony acting relatives that barely knew my name, but this time I would be traveling for a very good cause. My older brother Chad, who usually accompanied me on the agonizing journey, couldn't make it this year thank God. He and my father were in the middle of fighting some legal battle concerning the family business so I gladly traveled alone.

The best part of flying across the country this year was knowing that when I got back I would be "the shit". Jenny found a way to work around my father's stingy pockets. She happened to be dating one of California's top plastic surgeons and he agreed to work on me if I did the same little favor Chad customarily did for them. If I didn't say yes where else was I going to get the $7,000 it would cost for the operation?

During the majority of the flight we experienced major turbulence. I was a nervous wreck on the plane, guzzling little bottles of Gin and praying that we didn't crash. Reading about the pros and cons of cosmetic surgery helped keep me calm and focused. Before landing in Los Angeles, I managed to sneak in the last few sips of Gin and by the time we arrived I was quite exhilarated, having long forgotten any nervousness.

After the other strenuous ordeal of claiming my baggage, I walked out of LAX airport holding authentic Louis Vuitton luggage at my side. Just imagine my appearance that of the average white girl on vacation. No one suspected that I was carrying over $150,000 worth of drugs in my bag.

Just as she said she would, Jenny was waiting outside and welcomed me with an ice-cold Corona. In return, I greeted her with the same fake ass kiss on the cheek and kept it moving. My sister hadn't changed at all. Jenny was the same money hungry floozy that she was before college.

"You got my shit?" Jenny asked right away, "cause if you don't you can get your behind right back on the plane."

"It's in my bag bitch damn, can I at least get in the fucking car first nice to see you too."

I flicked my cigarette to the ground before handing over the product. The favor I owed was simple. All I had to do was smuggle some designer drugs on the plane and everything after that would be taken care of. Cool. I felt the chances of getting caught by airport security were slim, because who would search a little innocent looking white girl like me?

"Guess how much money these little shits are worth?" Jenny stared in awe as she held one of the glass containers between her finger and thumb, "fifteen big ones baby!"

"A piece?" I questioned strangely.

"That's right fifteen thousand dollars a piece... you did good kid."

"To me they look like little bottles of urine what is it?"

Even though Jenny was wild and all that, she still had a strange geeky side. In high school she once sold her own estrogen to fertility clinics just to go on a trip with her friends when my father refused to pay for it. There was no telling what was in those bottles and I didn't really care as long as I got what I wanted.

"Obviously, you don't keep up with the latest trends my dear... its DMT" Jenny stated simply.

I looked at her expressionless like I was supposed to really know what that was.

"Daddy's an undertaker and you never heard of Dimethyltryptamine? It's brain fluid stupid! Sometimes I think you were adopted."

I didn't know what in the hell she was talking about, but played along like I totally understood. Jenny put in plain words that my brother Chad, who worked as an anesthesiologist, unlawfully extracted spinal fluid from pregnant women during their epidural procedures. He then mixed it with Dimethyltryptamine he took from dead bodies in daddy's mortuary. Jenny sold the precious extract all over southern California to wealthy actors and musicians for big doe. It was the new craze in Hollywood and her doctor friend loved the shit.

"I'm not gonna waste my time explaining to an idiot like you every medical detail of how and why it happens," Jenny flipped her hair back, "but when DMT is injected into the blood stream you can experience some genetic memory of the person it was extracted from as it enters your Hypothalamus gland... wanna' try some!"

"Sure why not? Does daddy know anything about this?" I asked, at the same time scanning the parking lot to see if anyone was nearby.

"Why do you think he's being sued Jaz? Daddy's been selling body parts on the black market for years" Jenny made a face as she carefully filled the syringe, "okay just be still this is gonna pinch a little."

Jenny placed the needle to my forearm crease as I held a tourniquet around my bicep to pop out a vein. I looked away in repulsion as she carefully injected the dose of DMT into my blood stream. In seconds I was nodding like that drug addict in front of Kayla's apartment. I experienced the most euphoric high ever. I felt like I was on mushrooms, X and acid all at once.

When we pulled off in her boyfriend's Aston Martin, Jenny downed her Corona while the summer breeze blew through her luxurious blonde hair. Since Jenny was into club music nowadays, she blasted her favorite Techno CD the whole time we zoomed 100mph down the expressway. You would never know she used to be a hardcore hip-hop fan.

It was my father's wishes that I stay with my grandmother in Beverly Hills, but I would have rather slept on a goddamn park bench than spend another fucking summer with the snobby crypt keeper and her musty ass. That idea was out. I was staying with Jenny in Santa Monica for the summer whether my father liked it or not.

By the time we pulled up to Jenny's beachfront

condo we noticed that some of her friends had already started a bon fire near the shoreline. They were jumping around like drunken hooligans at a hockey game and a party was the last thing I needed. I was exhausted from the nerve-racking flight, but I could see that sleeping was out of the equation.

Jenny's friends were dressed straight out of an Abercrombie & Fitch catalog. They all wore dingy looking T-shirts with filthy flip-flops, as if it was stylish to look dirty. There wasn't one guy there my type, but in the midst of strangers chugging down beers and smoking bongs, I eventually socialized instead of crashing on the couch.

The party lasted all weekend. When I woke up two days later I had a throbbing headache. Between all the 151 vodka shots, pills and garbage weed, I had a fucking migraine out of this world. Empty beer bottles and grease stained pizza boxes were left everywhere, so I had to kick my way through trash just to get to the bathroom. Staring into the mirror for twenty minutes I examining my unsightly body. The huge mirrors and big bulb dressing room lights that decorated Jenny's bathroom, revealed every detailed flaw on my skin. I felt so ugly that I couldn't even look at myself for too long.

"Mommy has a surprise for you two" I spoke softly to my A-cup size breasts like they were kids, "soon mommy will be able to kiss you two good night."

After taking a long hot shower I got dressed excited for my big day. I had a bag already packed with all the essentials one would want to have with them for a short stay in the hospital.

"Jenny wake up I don't wanna be late... Jennieee," I whined, while jingling her car keys next to her ear, "wake up wake up wake uhh-up."

"What time is it?" Jenny snatched the keys from my hand with her eyes still closed, "just give me five more minutes I'm begging you please."

My appointment wasn't scheduled until 10 A.M, but I wanted to get there early. After forcing Jenny to brush her teeth, I slid my big sis her Gucci slippers and we hit the highway. Whereas most people drank coffee in the morning to get going, Jenny had another way of perking up. She drove slowly down Wilshire Boulevard in Beverly Hills sniffing lines of coke in between sentences.

"You know Jaz," Jenny snorted twice, "if you go too big you're going to have terrible backaches," she warned before one long sniff.

Jenny tried talking me out of getting large implants even though she had just got her already huge implants re-enlarged three months ago. I wasn't listening to a word she said. I was too nervous that the police were going to pull us over and just nodded like a bobble head doll the entire time.

When we got to where we were going I took a deep breath as we walked into the fancy looking doctors office. Since it was still early we were the only people there besides the doctor and his staff. Jenny sat with me in the waiting room flipping through photo albums of previous patients to get an idea of what breast sizes would look best on me. I didn't need her stank breath opinion and ignored her once again.

"You must be the lovely Jasmine," welcomed Doctor Crowley, while I sat there scanning the Essence best sellers list, "Jenny has told me so much about you," he said, "why don't you come with me so we can go over some preliminary measures."

Jenny had been sleeping with this 40- year old cornball for months. He wasn't the most handsome guy in the world, but he was a board certified plastic surgeon, which says it all. Jenny was trading pussy for perks. Who wouldn't like trips to Hawaii for lunch and shopping sprees on Rodeo drive every week?

Doctor Crowley acted so mannerly in front of his staff, but when he closed his office door his whole style changed. One minute he's acting like Mr. Rogers, than the next he's acting like Robert Downey, Jr. on crack. I couldn't quite figure him out.

"You got my shit?" Doctor Crowley asked Jenny as soon as the door shut, "'cause if you don't you can walk your ass right out this office."

"It's in my bag Al, relax honey."

In exchange for the bottles Jenny handed over, Doctor Crowley handed me some paperwork to sign, which I happily did right away. He didn't even look the papers over.

"Now that we're all settled you can come this way," he winked after squeezing my behind with both hands, "I'll have you prepped and ready to go in no time."

I showed Doctor Crowley the picture I kept of Kayla to explain how I wanted to look before stripping down to nothing in the examination room.

"Can you give me a body like this?" I asked, sharing the photo and pointing out areas of interest.

"I'm not god, but I'm the best in the business" He replied self-assuredly.

Ten minutes later, after the nurses sterilized my entire body, Doctor Crowley rolled me into the operating room his self. I relaxed on the gurney table ready for a complete transformation.

"*We'll cut here and over here,*" he spoke to his staff, while using a surgical marker to line the first incision.

Buck Fifty

"You won't feel a thing sweetie, just relax and take a deep breath," said the nursing assistant as she placed the anesthesia gas mask to my face, "think happy thoughts and when you open your eyes you'll look absolutely wonderful."

Dangerous Curves

I slept hours after the operation and felt groggy and dizzy when I came to. My curiosity and excitement gave me the strength to make it to a mirror. I couldn't stop smiling at what I observed as I stood in the lavatory saying damn to myself. My chest jumped from a mosquito bite A-cup, to a voluptuous 38-DD. My new melons were so perfectly round and succulent now. I loved them. Whoever said money can't buy you happiness was probably a broke son of a bitch with no imagination.

Prior to surgery my lips were thin and dry looking, but gratefully, the collagen shots inflated them to the likeness of Angelina Jolie's luscious kisser. There was a lot of soreness and numbing pain to endure, but after a few Vitamin C tablets and Pineapple extract, the swelling would stop in no time, the doctor said. Growing up in Fairfield, I was duped into believing that all men liked slim trim blonde gals with small lips and slender bottoms, but as I ventured out into the world I hadn't seen a black woman yet, with a weave and a big bubble ass lack attention or suffer with any dating problems.

Big bootys seemed to mesmerize men of all races. Oh how I wanted them to gawk at my ass too. I wanted them to shift their crotches and snap their necks like they did when Kayla walked pass. For that reason I decided to have the state of the art gluteoplasty (butt enhancement) performed, regardless of its yearly upkeep. If I had to have other people's beef stuffed in my body just to have a nice onion, then that's what I had to do.

Overweight women get liposuctions all the time, whereas the doctor removes the fat, but with this state of the art procedure I had done on me, the doctor actually fills you up with other peoples unwanted fat cells after they filter it of course. I know it sounds nasty but according to research, micro fat grafting was the safest and most natural way to get a gluteoplasty and the rejection rate was low.

I even read some brochures in the doctor's office that surprisingly gave a complete history of the black woman's rotund derriere. I learned that African women, with *Steatopygia,* a condition of particularly protuberant buttocks, were envied even centuries ago all throughout Europe. Their shocking curves caused much discussion and back then, any fashionable white woman wore a bustle skirt just to give off the appearance that she was holding junk in her trunk like the African chicks.

In May of 1810, an English soldier and a farmer from South Africa arrived in London with an exotic import: a young black girl named Saartjie Baartman. Her overly endowed butt cheeks, which were common among the Khoikhoi people of South Africa, created a craze throughout all of Europe. Venus Hottentot as they named Saartjie, was paraded in a sideshow circus where people paid two shillings to watch her pace around a tiny stage and afterward have their way with her.

A butt like Saartjie was unheard of in Europe. Her backside was so mesmerizing to the white people of that time, that after she mysteriously died at the age of 26, her remains (buttocks) were dismembered and put on display at Paris' Museë de L'Homme until the 1970's. Basically I was just repeating history by trying to mimic Kayla. As a white girl I knew the power of the booty and I wanted to share in its profound effect on men.

Anyhow, Doctor Crowley filled each cheek with 1800cc of pure fat, which is about 10 pounds in total added to my gluteus maximus. Before the stunning enhancement you could have ironed your clothes on my ass, but now I had something globular. There was only one catch though. At my young age it was more than likely that my body would reabsorb the new fat cells, so I would need to get refills every few years or so to keep up its plump appearance.

For the rest of the summer I let my aching body recoup until it was almost time to fly back to Connecticut. I read juicy street novels and window-shopped online everyday to pass the time. My last two days in California were spent real-life shopping on Rodeo drive and if we had enough time left I wanted to work on my tan at the beach. I was out of my league shopping with Jenny though. Baby Phat and Rocawear were the brands I preferred, but fucking around with her I ended up overdosing on Gucci and Roberto Cavalli. I needed an entirely new wardrobe cause none of my bras or draws fit anymore. I used to take a size 8 in jeans, but now my new rump demanded a 14, which was a problem I enjoyed.

"Ooh look at this one," Jenny uttered, as I shook my head at the outrageous price tag, "Al will cum on himself if he sees me in this shit!"

The mannequin we stood in front of displayed a Gucci g-string on its bum similar to dental floss.

"Why wear anything at all?" I laughed, "I got a ball of string at home you could use instead of spending your money on that."

As much as I wanted to flaunt my new body on the sand, I had no choice but to hit the tanning salon with the short amount of time I had left before the flight. Artificial sunrays darkened my chalky white skin, but always left me with more of an orangey type of appearance. There was no way I could go back home looking like a freaking carrot, so Jenny took me to the most posh day spa in Beverly Hills to get a Mystic tan. Instead of using artificial light, they sprayed my entire body with melatonin paint, which gave my skin a tone of light bronze.

"What'chu think Jen," I spun around after the cashier handed back my father's credit card, "do I look fucking hot or what!"

"Damn that shit sucks," Jenny clicked off her cell phone and shook her head in disbelief.

"What's wrong? You think I'm too dark?" I frowned.

"No you look great... it's not you, it's daddy. That was Chad on the phone. He said they lost the case."

"So what?" I shook my shoulders like I didn't care, "forget about daddy and let's finish shopping!"

"What do you mean so what? Business has been good selling what I sell and further more those people were suing daddy for over a million dollars. You better act more concerned than *so what*, cause that means you're broke now too stupid!"

Problems stay, but money comes and goes. Besides having to pay the 1.3 million in punitive damages for accidentally cremating a few bodies that were supposed to be embalmed, Chad said the judge ordered a further criminal investigation into my father's shady business affairs.

Realizing how serious the matter was I started getting upset. Jenny was more nonchalant, because all of her things, like the new condo and tuition were paid for already. Plus she had her pussy-whipped boyfriend doctor to take care of her. I didn't even own a car yet and basically I lived off of my father's credit cards. I was SOL: shit outta' luck.

"What am I gonna do?" I sniveled, in between wiping tears from my lip, "I'm allergic to broke what am I gonna do Jenny?"

"Well at least you got new tits!" Jenny teased, as she bobbled my breasts, "*I can see it now* we can make a fortune in Vegas as the double-D debutantes."

"You're not funny. Do you think grandma would help daddy out with some money if he asked?" I questioned in desperation.

"I seriously doubt it. Not after what happened to mommy," Jenny smirked, "I really don't think so. Grandma blames him for mommy's death... well I'm just glad I moved out here when I did," Jenny said as we hugged goodbye.

See at one time my father was one of the wealthiest morticians in Connecticut until his heavy drinking destroyed his reputation. Marrying my mother resuscitated his career, but when she died her blue blood money left right along with her.

Here I was supposed to be feeling good boarding the plane with my new look and all, but actually I felt rather depressed. By the way Jenny was talking I was probably going to have to get a job. There was no way in hell I was going to spend my days asking people if they wanted paper or plastic. God meant me to push a Bentley, not push a broom. I had to come up with something.

After landing safely in Connecticut, at Tweed airport, I waited almost two hours for my father to pick me up. When he finally got there I was in the middle of exchanging numbers with this cute cabbie I had just met and daddy flipped the fuck out.

"I'm going to tell you this once and once only," he reprimanded while yanking me through the Airport like a kid, "If I ever catch you talking to one of those head rag niggers again you'll be sorry! Do you understand me Jasmine!"

I hated the way my father said my name. Everyone else called me Jaz, but he had to always call me Jasmine. He was getting on my last nerve I swear.

"Whatever daddy why you trippin'?" I sucked my teeth when he ripped the phone number up in my face, "we were just talking damn!"

Daddy slapped me for talking back to him and didn't say a word about my obvious enhancements or even ask me how my vacation or flight was. He was in a real shitty mood and it showed. I hadn't seen him get this upset in years.

As we were waiting at the light a brand new Mercedes pulled up alongside of us blasting Hot 97. It was filled with black guys nodding their head to the music.

"I don't know what happened to this country," my father heaved a sigh, "Niggers used to shine shoes for a nickel and tap dance for a penny, now look at those sons a bitches in their fancy cars."

I kept my mouth shut this time.

"I'm sorry if I've been taking things out on you Jasmine, but as you probably already know we lost the case. That means I have no choice but to start clamping down on spending. I cancelled most of my credit cards and we have to probably move out of the house soon."

"Why? Did you lose the house too?"

"*Those goddamn courts and their bullshit laws,*" my father thought out loud as the Benz pulled off, "No I didn't lose the house, but if I don't pay them fast enough they'll try to take that from me too I'm sure."

"Am I still going to Laurelton next semester?" I asked, hoping no was the answer.

"Well not until I get back on my feet we can't afford it right now I'm sorry."

I shook my head like I was mad, but inside I was jumping for joy. I hated that all girls school anyway. I couldn't wait to go to a normal school that at least had boys in it.

Daddy Dearest

By the time it came around to go back to school in September, we were living in a neglected section of Bridgeport. I now understood the saying *be careful what you wish for.* Daddy sold the house in Fairfield along with some other property he owned, just to pay off the lawsuit. Our new location was nice, if you consider sharing space with dead bodies enjoyable. One of my father's childhood friends gave him a next to nothing price on an old funeral home a hairsbreadth away from a cemetery. I guess the reason he agreed to take it was in hopes of starting his business all over again.

My pride was shattered I must say, but Bridgeport was nothing like Fairfield. It was off the chain live! Never could I purchase a bag of weed in the same store where I bought toilet paper and pads.

Unlike my old hood, where black people were rarely seen outside after dark, people in Bridgeport stood on the corners playing loud music until all hours of the night. Gunshots rang out on a regular basis and sometimes I even heard people running through our backyard escaping the police.

After a useless lecture from my father about the decaying public school system, he decided to enroll me in Bassick High School based on the convenient proximity to the house. Opposite to Laurelton Prep, Bassick had a demographics ratio of 2% white. From being around Kayla I had already knew a few people who went to Bassick and I couldn't wait to see the look on their faces when they seen how big my lady humps flourished over the summer.

As I stepped off the school bus with my head held high, my breasts bounced with buoyancy all the way to the entrance. Yeah there were some other chicks in the hall with nice bodies and all that, but regardless of what they had I was the new chick in school and all eyes were on me. Everybody always wants the new girl because the new girl is a mystery.

When I spotted one of Kayla's friends in the hall talking with some other girls, I waved from afar so she could see me.

"Yo, Nikki what's up, come holla' at ya' girl!" I shouted.

I was excited to see Nikki and ask about how Kayla was doing, but it took her some time to acknowledge me. She looked me dead in the face and just turned her head. I expected other bitches to throw salt in my game the first day, but not Nikki. We were supposed to be cool and the gang. When Nikki finally came over to where I stood it was almost time for homeroom.

"I thought that was you I saw getting off the bus this morning," Nikki snickered, "what happened to the Benz? What happened to *I got this I got that*?"

Nikki sounded real bitter. I couldn't understand why she was trying to ridicule me after all of the clubs we hit together, not to mention the late night phone conversations when she needed someone to talk to.

"What's up with you Nikki? Why you acting funny?" I rolled my eyes at the pack of ugly girls standing behind her.

Nikki's friends made a circle around us like they wanted to jump me.

"*We should fuck this white bitch up*!" the small crowd roared with racial slurs.

The next thing I know somebody punched me in the face before the security guard broke it up. Nikki walked away without saying anything else to me. I found out later that the girl who socked me was Nikki's cousin. She was the one that had a baby with Manny, the pest who called my house from prison.

"Oh its like that Nik?" I stood alone waiting for an answer, "I thought we were cool?"

"Yeah bitch its like dat!" Nikki replied as the crowd dispersed, "leave Tariq the hell alone or we'll jump your ass everyday until you get the message!"

When I got off the bus earlier that morning, I ran into this blazing hottie name Tariq. I met Tariq at a party while hanging out with Kayla last year. I knew Nikki liked him, but I had no clue they were a couple now, so when I spotted him we hugged and kicked it like two people who hadn't seen each other in awhile would do. Someone must have seen us and told Nikki that I was all up in her man's face. Nikki was right suspecting I wanted to do her man, but I never pushed up on him out of respect. Since she wanted to play me around her little friends, I felt like fuck her respect! I was on a mission now to ride her man.

With my scandalous charm and porn size tits, I knew I could scoop Tariq with the quickness. Tariq and I shared most of the same classes, so we were able to converse plenty. After talking on the phone for a couple of days, I enticed Tariq to ditch his last two periods and sneak with me to my crib. On the way to my house Tariq confessed that he was kind of a virgin. He said that Nikki made him wait four months before she even let him feel on her. When he told me that, the thought of fresh meat popped into my mind. I licked my lips like a vampire getting ready to taste fresh blood.

It was obvious to me that Tariq's only reason for skipping school was to break his virginity, but who cares about feelings when you just wanna get in somebody's pants. Given the fact that so many black girls, including Nikki, acted stingy with their mouths, I got hip to the head game early and have been swallowing ever since.

Granting good head was a secret us white girls from the suburbs used to steal inner-city dudes away from their chicks. I learned how to go down on a man from listening to my sister when we were little.

"*The key is to make it wet,*" Jenny shared her expertise when I was ten, "*spit on it like you're mad at the dick and always make loud slurping noises while you suck... they love that shit!*"

As soon as we got to the basement I ripped open my shirt. Tariq was in amazement at how big my breasts were now compared to the first time we met. I let him ogle for a minute, before pulling his head into my chest. Tariq got so hard that I thought his dick was going to shoot off from his body and fly around the room like a rocket. I teased him in the beginning slowly licking his meat like a chocolate icicle, and then slobbered away as I played with myself at the same time.

"Who was that? You said nobody was home?" Tariq whispered in concern as my head went up and down, "Is somebody upstairs?" He nervously asked.

Suddenly the basement door flew open. The rapid bang of the door slamming against the wall startled both of us. I froze as the sound of scampering feet rushed down the steps. Tariq stood up in shock with his pants at his ankles, while my father now stood in the basement with us. Daddy reeked of liquor. Out of nowhere he grabbed a small pipe wrench and whacked Tariq in the head with it.

"The only niggers I'll have in this house goddamn it, are DEAD NIGGERS!" he slurred, before striking Tariq once more.

Tariq's head was split open. He fell backwards putting up a fight, but daddy grew stronger and restrained him very easily. I cried in fear as my father ripped off my panty hose. He used them to tie Tariq's wrists to a cast iron pipe that spanned across the basement ceiling. Tariq was in a state of terror and could barley plead for my assistance. He just moaned in pain looking somewhat dazed calling for my help.

I didn't know what my father was up to, but he had the same crazy look in his eye as he did the day at the airport.

"Call the police!" Tariq shouted with the last bit of energy he had, as my father spread his butt cheeks apart.

By now I had stopped crying. I stared at my father in shock as he brutally raped a teenage boy in front of his daughter.

"Thought you could screw my little girl!" He

hollered with each stroke, “How does it feel with a dick up *YOUR* ass! I lost everything because of you fucking niggers!”

“What are you doing daddy stop!” I cried out, “stop you’re hurting him! Stop!”

My father just looked at me with a soulless stare, revealing the evil spirits that possessed his mind. I knew I should’ve helped Tariq, like call the police or something, but I couldn’t find the strength to move. I was too petrified. Tariq’s horrid screams faded. I think he even shit on himself cause I could smell a foul odor.

“I’ll teach you both a lesson that you’ll never forget,” my father snapped in a sharp Irish accent, “you’re just like your mother Jasmine… you disobeyed me. I told you what I’d do if I ever caught you with one of these jungle bunnies again get over here!”

The taste of blood and shit almost made me puke and this was the first time I had a prick in my mouth that I didn’t enjoy. In the most deranged manner my father rubbed his sperm into my skin as if it was Noxzema, then slapped me with his penis back and forth east to west.

Tariq cried silently as blood dripped from his torn anal canal down his leg.

“You made me do this,” my father hollered out of breath, “you should’ve listened to me, now go to your room!”

I ran upstairs crying uncontrollably, with a hatred for my father that I thought I’d never have.

BK

While I was dealing with the stuff I was going through, Kayla had dropped out of high school and enrolled herself into the school of hard knocks. She had been living in the East New York section of Brooklyn, with this guy named Johnny Red while her pops did his bid. Red was somewhat of an uncle to Kayla. Her father left instructions for Red to look out for his daughter after he got word in prison that his sister was strung out on base. It was a shame how dearly Kayla missed and loved her father, but I wish I could say the same about mine.

The woman who was originally supposed to take care of Kayla could barely take care of herself. Kayla's aunt Gina was only 26 years old with a boyfriend for everyday of the week. She was into sniffing coke and hitting the clubs and Gina didn't give a shit about her niece's rearing and safety. It was obvious that the only reason she agreed to take Kayla in was for the money.

Instead of using the funds Kayla's father provided to take care of his daughter, Gina wasted the doe on drugs of course. She had graduated from coke to crack over the years and before long became a full-fledged base head. Gina would stay out all night suckin' and fuckin' for a ten second high, while Kayla roamed the projects getting in trouble.

Kayla's father never made it home from prison I'm sad to say. Three years into his sentence he died from a subtle disease brought on by the *Agent Orange* chemicals used in the Vietnam War. Kayla was heartbroken, but only mourned for a short time. She understood death very well and was sure that her mother and father would be reunited in the spiritual realm. To depart from this life protecting the people you love is the true warrior's premise and Kayla's father was a true warrior no doubt.

People gathered in droves surrounding her dad's ultimate resting place at the Evergreen Cemetery in Brooklyn. Standing tall at the funeral service were terribly aged Vietnam veterans, most in their 50's and 60's positioned in the vein of honor guards. For his final send off, a local jazz band blew shiny brass horns and trumpets. Their instruments blared with melodic intensity as the birds in nearby trees flew away in unison, after a loud 21 gun salutation.

Kayla's eyes filled with tears, but she still stood firm. Johnny Red consoled her tightly as the men lowered her pops' casket into the Earth. Kayla stared off into the sky assessing the lives of her parents who were buried side by side.

After the lengthy service concluded Kayla and her Aunt Gina exited a complementary limousine in front of a public storage building. All beefs were put on hold. Kayla agreed to let Gina help her go through the stuff her father kept in storage before he went to jail. Gina helped for a minute, but as soon as she found a few dollars in her brother's old army jacket pocket she headed out the door.

"I'll be back in a minute," Gina claimed, "I need me a cigarette."

"Whateva," Kayla thoughtlessly responded, while looking through the cardboard boxes deciding what and what not to keep.

Gina vanished as soon as she got outside. Hours later, after going through everything by herself, Kayla decided to find Gina and curse her out for not helping like she promised. Kayla had a good idea where Gina was, so she took a dollar van to the Van Dyke housing projects. Just as the Econoline dropped her off, Kayla spotted Gina walking away from a group of poison pushers that were gathered by the benches. Gina walked into one of the buildings and disappeared once again. Kayla was heated. She still had a key to her aunt's apartment, so she went upstairs and decided to wait for her.

Twenty minutes went by and still no sign of Gina. Kayla felt like she was wasting her time on a lost cause, so she decided to bounce. By the time Kayla had got down to the 3rd floor steps, an echoed voice could be heard. Kayla recognized Gina's voice and became totally enraged like never before.

"C'mon man let me get the two for nine and I owe you ten for the other two," Gina pleaded.

"Fuck dat you already owe me," the dealer said, "I don't give a shit if your brother was buried today or yesterday I need my money now! If you want this crack you betta get on your knees and earn the last two!

And if you're good maybe, just maybe I'll let what you owe me slide."

Kayla was infuriated and the disrespect coming from dude's mouth made it worse. Gina agreed to suck the nigga off on the staircase in return for two more of them things. Kayla reached in her pocket and pulled out an old school straight razor her father used to shave with that she found in storage. Neither the drug dealer nor Gina, who was kneeling on the dirty cement steps, heard Kayla creep down from behind.

The obnoxious trick was looking down at Gina with his hands on his waist commanding Gina how to pleasure him. While Gina slurped and burped funky balls and dick, Kayla pulled the dealer's head back. She wrapped his long braids around her palm then ferociously slit his throat. In the blink of an eye, blood poured forth from the man's neck onto Gina's head like a cheap horror movie. The young man convulsed himself down the steps as Gina stared in shock from all the blood.

"Oh my fuckin' gawd!" she shrieked as her pusher lay there shaking, "What da fuck! Oh shit!"

Kayla silenced Gina's ear piercing screams by covering her mouth with the keepsake American flag they gave her at the funeral. Gina looked around franticly, in fear that someone might've seen what happen.

In seconds the dealer was dead with his eyes bulging out his head. Kayla gave Gina a stare of disappointment before she spat in her aunt's face. She walked gallantly up the steps like nothing even happened. Being the hopeless crack head that she was, Gina went through the dealers' pockets. She stuffed a sandwich bag of crack into her dingy dress before rushing up the stairs behind Kayla.

"You must have lost your goddamn mind child! Did you know who you just killed?" Gina rambled after taking a nervous hit from her crack pipe, "Day gonna' kill us ya heard me day gonna' kills us!" Gina repeated as the crack paranoia set in more.

"Whose gonna kill us?" Kayla said as she washed the blood off the white porcelain sink, "Nobody cares what happens around here, not you, not them, NOBODY CARES!"

Kayla slapped the pipe out of Gina's mouth as tears ran down both of their faces.

"Drugs destroyed our entire family in some way or another can't you see that! I hope you choke on the next dick you suck for them! Get the hell out of my way!"

Gina bent down to pick up the glass stem that her niece knocked onto the floor, then sat in the corner hopelessly flicking her lighter. Kayla was halfway out the door before she turned around to look at Gina one last time.

"I never told you this before," Kayla confessed as she stood under the threshold, "but I wanted to be just like you when I was little. Now you make me sick! I hope one day when you're lying in the gutta' all high and shit you realize you had a niece and a family that loved you."

As Kayla closed the door Gina began to burst out in tears. When she couldn't get her lighter to work, she flung her precious crack pipe in frustration. Ironically as the pipe shattered against the wall in a thousand pieces, someone else's aunt was beaming up successfully on the other side of that wall.

The dealer's body was still lying in the stairwell as Kayla jogged down the steps. She stepped over his lifeless shadow and kept it moving. To her he deserved to die. Not good people like her mother and father.

Kayla wandered the streets contemplating her next move. When nightfall drew she headed over to Johnny Reds'. Once there, Kayla dropped her bags with a desperate look. She needed to exhale the fire from her lungs and sit down.

"I miss my family so much," Kayla let out a deep breath, "I had a big fight with Gina and I did something terrible Red... I..."

Before Kayla could explain the rest of the story, Red hugged her tightly then helped her with her bags. Red didn't need to know what happened. He watched Kayla grow up and loved her like his own. Over the years he witnessed how ill mannered Gina treated Kayla and foreseen the tribulations heading Kayla's way.

During that awful humid night, Kayla and Red talked until the sun came up. He shared stories with Kayla about her father in Vietnam, and she told him stories about her friends in Connecticut. I had my own stories to share, with whom, I did not know?

Rest In Piss

It felt like it took forever, but the day finally came for me to graduate. I was one step closer to living on my own. Seven miserable months had passed since that traumatic Halloween afternoon in the basement, and no matter how much time went by, everyday felt the same. I was an emotional mess. As it turned out, Tariq was very active in sports, so when he turned up missing, posters went up everywhere. I even saw his face on a milk carton once.

I felt blameworthy about Tariq's callous death and to escape all the guilt built up inside, I got high everyday like Styles P. My drug habit skyrocketed faster than the price of gas. Cocaine was my new love. Any love I had in the past for my father was a vague memory. To me he was a dead man walking.

It was common now for my heavily intoxicated

father to walk passed my bedroom door masturbating, while I did my homework. I was petrified of being in the house with him alone because he was fucking crazy for real for real. To avoid further incestual encounters, I started hanging in local bars, where I stayed out all night long. Whenever I had the choice between sleeping with someone I met at the bar or going home to my father, I chose the stranger. In a matter of months I slept with practically the entire Westside just to avoid coming home. That's probably how I caught crabs three times in a row. I sucked so much dick in the hood I earned the nickname 'fuck face'. The road I was heading down was not a good look.

My nights were restless sleeping in a stranger's bed. Tariq's haunting screams replicated in my mind on a daily basis. I never told anyone what happened to Tariq and it was killing me to let someone know how I was feeling. If I told Nikki what I knew, she would beat my ass and call the police. I couldn't take it anymore. I had to tell somebody something or I was going to go nuts just like my father.

I ran to my brother Chad, who showed me just how much he really cared. Chad was fresh out of that DMT shit when I asked for some, so he gave me a shot of Thorazine instead. When I calmed down I told him exactly what happened and he twisted everything like it was my fault.

"Do you think I would turn my own father in over some nigger you fucked?" Chad shouted offensively, "If you stayed with your own kind none of this would've happened!"

Chad didn't give a shit about what my father did. He would have probably done the same thing. Chad was just as racist as my father and he just wanted to know if I had anal sex with Tariq. When I was ten years old Chad made me promise that I would never let anyone else penetrate me anally. He said it would be his special place and gift to him as his half sister. I never counted Chad as being my first, so to me I was still a virgin until James hit it.

"Is my ass and who's been fucking it the only thing you care about?" I replied with much anger, "I thought I could come to you for comfort but you're just like daddy... fuck you Chad!"

"Well you obviously thought wrong sis," Chad retorted with a cynical comeback.

"Well *maybe* I should tell the police what you've been doing with dead people's body fluids and how you smuggle drugs back and forth to California or *maybe* I should tell your girlfriend about all the times you molested me growing up! How 'bout that?"

"You listen to me you little whore! I've been good to you all these years. You loved having sex with me so don't even try it. If you tell anyone about my thing in California I'll kill you myself," Chad gritted his teeth, "do I make myself clear Jaz?"

Chad was all talk and no action. He was a skinny geek that never won a fistfight in his life and I knew I could kick his ass if he took it any further. When he grabbed my arm I backslapped him like a five-dollar trick on the first of the month before leaving him holding his cheek.

As soon as I got back to Bridgeport I walked to the liquor store two blocks from my house. I almost lost a track of time downing Heinekens and doing lines. I forgot I had to get ready for my high school graduation.

The graduation had started at 5pm and it was already 5:30 so I didn't want to miss the whole thing. Being the big time tease that I was, on top of being tipsy, I decided to only wear a bra and thong panties under my lightweight graduation gown. Luckily I arrived at the ceremony only minutes before my name was called. The last diploma was handed out and everyone threw their square caps in the air, screaming like cowboys.

"Fuck the world," were my exact sentiments if I recall correctly, *"I don't need nobody!"*

The only person that I did miss was my mother. I wished she were there that day to share in my joy. I knew out of anyone she would know how I felt about life.

As I made my way outside, all types of guys gave me hugs. Some rubbed up against my body detecting that I was half naked under the thin rayon gown. Others had the nerve to grab my ass like they knew me and of course the ones I slept with already asked me to go to their graduation parties. I declined each tempting offer and decided to keep it simple, even though I was high, hot and horny.

Instead of letting the fellas run a train on me that night, I just hung out in Marina Village with some girls from my homeroom. We got high and talked shit about all of our former classmates and teachers that we didn't like, then broke off for the night.

While walking the long way home, I cringed as a billboard size poster of Tariq in his football uniform caught my attention. The peeling billboard attached to the side of a gas station read, *"If anyone has seen this person please call 1-800-missing."*

My high was completely blown and for some reason I became enraged, breaking bottles and keying cars as I staggered home. When I finally reached the door it was almost 3 o'clock in the morning. I tried to creep inside through the back door, but it sounded like my father was still up arguing with somebody in the living room. My curiosity would not let me go upstairs so I stayed in the kitchen to listen.

The next thing I heard was glass break then a lamp fell to the floor. I peeked my head around the entrance to see who my father was talking to and oddly enough it was an old picture of my mother that he held. The glass in the frame had shattered and being much more wasted than I was, he didn't even realize that his hand was bleeding.

"*...Since you and your daughter like sleeping with monkeys! I'm going to kill her too...*"

My heart dropped to a fetal position hesitant to function, as I overheard the truth about my mother's death. Daddy's drunken confession struck with such intensity that I couldn't move. As the vivid memory of my father ejaculating in my face flashed through my mind, so did every other demeaning incident in my life. Without explanation I placed a large Ginsu knife in my hand and pushed myself into the living room. I stood behind my father emotionless as I repeatedly drove the razor sharp blade into his back. I must have stabbed him over 25 times before I finally stopped.

All sounds muted as he fell face first crashing through the glass coffee table. I flipped him over to look into his eyes then bent down to kiss him as if he were my lover. I sucked the last bit of breath from my father's lungs like he did to my virtue. He was dead and there was no way he was coming back. I made sure of that.

For all these years my family and I were under the impression that my mother had died from a rare lead poisoning disease, but that night I learned the truth. The lead poisoning she suffered with was from the bullets my father fired into her chest when he caught her having sex with a black man from work. I felt like my mother's spirit used me to get revenge, and now she could rest in peace.

After doing a couple more lines of coke I fixed myself a sandwich before dragging the heavy bastard into the basement. My impulsive plan was to chop up his body like he made me help him do to Tariq, but it was easier said than done. There was broken glass and a thick pool of blood on the carpet that would have been impossible to get out, then another trail of blood all the way down to the basement. One good crime scene investigation would have easily got me busted.

"*What the fuck am I going to do*?" I thought, "*How can I make this look like an accident?*" I wondered pacing back and forth all night.

Around six in the morning I came up with the idea to burn down the entire goddamn house. I fumbled through the boxes of embalming fluid and other chemicals stored in the basement then thought a little harder.

"*I know, I'll make it look like he got drunk and started a fire while working with all these chemicals. Everyone knows daddy's a drunk and smokes cigars, it might work.*"

Before I set the blaze with one of my father's Cuban cigars, I rummaged through his wallet and removed all the cash he had, plus his two bankcards, before putting it back in his pants pocket. As the smoke began to seep upstairs from the basement, I stuffed my mother's picture on top of the clothes I quickly packed, then got the hell out of there even faster. I waited in the backyard watching the house burn from a distance, before calling 911 from a neighbor's house. The last words out of my mouth concerning my piece of shit father were R.I.P.

"Rest-In-Piss motherfucker!"

The next day, I sat in the police station blowing bubbles and popping chewing gum, while I waited in the station lobby. Chad was there and had already been questioned. Before Chad left the station he informed me that he was listed as the top beneficiary on daddy's life insurance policy and as soon as the check cleared, he'll give me my share if I kept my mouth shut about what I knew.

"Was Mr. O'Reilly involved with any hate groups?" Asked one of the detectives, *"Did he use or sell drugs to your understanding? At what time did you notice the house on fire?"* His partner inquired on and on and on.

This bullshit went on for about an hour. The investigators weren't charging me with nada they just wanted to question me about my father's business affairs. He was under investigation way before this. The detectives suspected that he was part of a white-collar ring that sold dead people's vital organs on the Internet and white market. If they were on to me about the fire they wouldn't be asking me questions about his work I figured.

I should have snitched on my brother to get him back for how he treated me days before, but I didn't. I had all the answers the police needed, but I kept my mouth shut mafia style.

"Oh one last thing Miss O'Reilly... were you planning a trip somewhere? Your neighbors stated that you had luggage or a bag with you when they answered the door? Do you always walk around with a month's supply of clothes in the middle of the night?"

"Yeah I do, I'm a runaway," I answered the cop, then asked, "are we finished I need some air?"

In a casual way the police let me know the fire seemed suspicious before they escorted me out. If my father's body didn't burn to ashes they might've had a case, but any idiot could see they were just grasping in the air for information.

Now that I was basically homeless I stayed at this rinky-dink motel until I could find a more stable place to live. My grandmother on my father's side lived in Mount Vernon, NY and she offered her extra bedroom to me, if I wanted to stay there, but I declined. My other Grandma, the stinky wrinkled rich one in California, asked me to live with her too, but when it came time to board the plane I conveniently missed the flight.

In two weeks I withdrew over $5000 using my father's debit cards at ATM machines. It was just about all he had following the lawsuit, but I made do with it. Nobody was going to stop me from doing things my way. This was my chance to be grown and live on my own. I figured if things didn't work out with my little ghetto adventure, I'll just move out to California with Jenny. It was that simple I thought. Oh, how wrong I was.

Duane Reade

A year had passed since I offed my pops and I hadn't shed a tear over his ass once. It was a typical Thursday morning in May and like any other time after my weekly Brazilian bikini waxing I hit *Chiffon's House of Glamour and Gossip*, the flyest beauty salon in Bridgeport. Chiffon's was unusually packed this particular day. High school girls were piling in to get dolled up for their proms, so it was a busy mess.

My brows needed trimming and my nails were starting to look a little roach too, but the real reason why I frequented the place so much was for the latest scoop. I learned things like who did who, who made the most money doing what in the streets, who was gay and best of all, who had the biggest dick in the hood.

For a white girl like me who wasted hours

watching rap videos to pick up style and slang, hanging out in Chiffon's was a 101 course in street savoir-faire. It was certainly the bomb spot to parlay in too, if you wanted to get known in the streets. Every woman in there was a ghetto superstar with drug dealing boyfriends, especially the beauticians. At this point I considered myself a star too, since I spent a fortune on stylish clothes and hung out with the beauty shop's owner.

As I walked through the door in a pair of tight Baby Phat jeans and my skimpy *Got Dick?* Print on my T-shirt, the door chime sounded announcing my entrance. Everyone paused to check out the new shiny bracelets on my arm before carrying on with their conversations. I received all types of jealous stares. My shit was straight blinging. I knew them chicks in there were jelly, because they all rolled their eyes in disgust. You get used to it after awhile, so I rolled my eyes right back at them before sitting down to get my refill.

"Girl...as long as I'm gettin' my sugar walls licked in the tropics I don't care how he makes his money," laughed one of the sassy beauticians, *"how many niggas around here ever took you to St. Lucia just to get some ass?"*

"Aren't you scared of gettin' arrested or even shot, messin' wit' dat' wild nigga?" A customer interjected, before her head was placed into the rinse sink.

"I ain't never scared!" Rita declared.

"I don't know about your man Rita, but my baby Duane knows not to mix his business with my pleasure. I'm a pro, not a hoe," Chiffon answered with a feminine three snaps up, three snaps down, *"you bitches need to read more learn more and change the globe wit' 'dat kitty kat."*

Chiffon Davis ran the place and out of all of the women in there she was the most restrained. I mean she could gossip with the best of them, but she was more laid back. Chiffon was that sexy conceited chick all the hustlers tried to get with. She had a body that wouldn't quit with an attitude to go with it. Most dudes were too scared to approach Chiffon because she was that beautiful. They figured what was the point in trying to get with someone who they knew would only turn them down.

For a short time I was involved with Chiffon's younger brother Breeze. Even though things didn't work out between Breeze and I, Chiffon never held a grudge against me and we stayed mad cool with each other. She taught me how to paralyze a man's mind game. Chiffon said tackle his strengths, rather than go after his weaknesses. If the guy looks good, make him feel like he's ugly. If he has a big dick, let him know that you had bigger. Even if you really haven't, she said lie about it cause in doing so, he'll feel like he has something to prove and you'll always have the upper hand.

Chiffon was like my personal street advisor and I was so jealous of her it wasn't even funny. Not of her looks and street smarts, but jealous of who she was engaged to. I always acted totally naïve around Chiffon and I let her believe what she wanted to believe to get closer to her man. I think she thought I was this dumb white girl with big titties who needed schooling. I guess that's why she took me under her wing like she did.

"So tell me," Sandy the nail technician asked a girl sitting next to me as she did my nails, "how did things go with you and my lil' cousin yesterday?"

"I should kick you in your damn mouth! That nigga had too many nots" the girl replied, "...not big enough, not hard enough and not paid enough and his breath smelled like shit on top of that!"

"Sandy? What did I tell you about hooking up my customers" Chiffon placed her hands on her hips as she stopped weaving a client's hair, "you really need to quit. How many times are you gonna try to set somebody up with those cornball cousins of yours? You're giving my business a bad name sweetie, come on get it together gurl."

"*I remember when Sandy tried to hook me up with her brother,*" a customer out of nowhere exclaimed, "*I come outside to meet the man right, and this silly ass nigga is wearin' headphones holding a bouquet of sky blue plastic roses! His car looked like it had cancer and the engine was all smokin' and shit. I ran back in the house and locked my damn door!*"

While silly laughter broke out inside the shop, the large storefront windows which proudly broadcast the name "Chiffon's House of Glamour and Gossip" in big audacious gold letters, began to vibrate from the pounding bass sounds of Smooth the Hustler and Trigga' the gambler's rap classic, *Broken Language.*

"*...The Glock cocker-The block locker- The rock chopper-The shot popper... The human drug generator-The honey gamer The chicken tricka'-The slicka' long dick pussy sticka'-The ready to bust that ass kicka'...*" blasted outside of Chiffon's salon, as a one of a kind custom made cherry drop top Range Rover pulled to the curb and parked.

Chiffon fixed her apron then threw a mint in her mouth for freshness. The entire salon grew quiet. The sexiest thug of the year hopped out draped in jewels. His broad shoulders filled out the crisp Banana Republic dress shirt that he wore and his jeans didn't hang off his ass like those of his workers. In spite of this, the heap of platinum chains and medallions around his neck overshadowed Duane's clean-cut appearance. Ironically Duane's last name was Read, and like *Duane Reade,* the popular chain of pharmacy stores in New York City, this Duane Read sold just as much narcotics as they did, maybe more.

Duane was the shit and he knew it. He walked through the door like he owned the place, because basically he did.

"Sup' ladies" the chocolate heartthrob greeted everyone, "where'd my favorite girl in the whole world disappear to that quick?"

Duane was obviously referring to Chiffon who had stepped in the back to get more hair.

"What did I tell you about blasting your music 'round here?" Chiffon complained as she re-entered the room, "this is a respectable business area baby and all that loud music shit is tacky."

Rather than jump into his arms and give the man a dynamic tongue kiss like anyone else would have done, Chiffon treated Duane indifferent with complaints. She even pushed his hand away when he attempted to pinch her ass.

"Stop playin' yo and give your man a kiss," Duane chuckled as he pulled his fiancé close, "I got something for you."

Chiffon opened the Littman jewelers bag then kissed Duane on the cheek. She tried on the diamond stick earrings in front of all the customers who just oooed and ahhed.

While the chatty employees and customers stayed in Duane's mouth listening to every word, I got up out my chair. Outside in the passenger seat sat one of Duane's lieutenants. He waved me out to the truck to talk, but I pointed at myself acting like I didn't know which girl he was referring to.

"Who Me?" I spoke silently through the window.

Wiz kept shaking his head yes as I continued to point at myself.

"Why don't you go see what he wants?" Duane said in his deep raspy voice, "Don't tell 'em I told you, but I think he wants to get with you."

"If Wiz had any class he would come in here and talk for himself," Chiffon intervened, "and since when did you become Cupid Duane?"

"Its okay Chiffon, as long as he's not related to Sandy," I shared a smile with Duane, "it's all good right!"

Sandy smacked her lips in repugnance as I switched my ass to the exit to meet Duane's friend. I leaned over the passenger side door to make it look like I was really interested in Wiz, but I really wanted Duane to get a good view of my booty poking out. Chiffon taught me that a girl could never go wrong in tight jeans and heels and she was right. I don't care if a man is with his wife or not, if you walk sexy in high heels and tight jeans he will find someway to check you out no matter what.

"How long do you think you can keep this shit up?" Wiz huffed at me.

"As long as we can," I shot back.

"I'm gettin' tired of this bullshit yo! My girl thinks I'm cheatin' on her ass cause of y'all," Wiz snapped again, "if Duane is so big and bad why don't he just come clean and let Chiffon know what time it is!"

"What do you know about game Wiz? Chiffon don't have a clue about me and Duane, so let her high and mighty ass think she's number one in his life," I laughed, "now smile cause everyone's looking at us."

I let Wiz slap me on the ass before I walked back

in the salon. From inside the shop it appeared like Wiz was the man I wanted. I laughed as if our conversation was charming, but the whole thing was a sham. I had been fucking Duane for months already. Matter of fact, Duane was the one who gave me the $3000 bangle bracelets on my arm that Chiffon complimented me on when I first walked in.

"Oh my god Wiz is so cute," I said as I sat back down in my chair, "he wants to take me out to eat... should I go with them?" I asked Chiffon.

"Them Who? Who else is in the car?" Chiffon responded suspiciously.

"No I mean *him*, should I go with Wiz to lunch was what I meant to say?"

"You told me you didn't like light skinned niggas, now all of a sudden you think Wiz is cute?"

I just shrugged my shoulders before Duane cut in.

"Bay, I hope you like your earrings. I gotta' go," Duane kissed Chiffon on the forehead, "call me if you need anything aw'right?"

"Where exactly out of town are you going?" Chiffon promptly inquired.

"Um... what's it called?" Duane pondered like a fool, "um?"

"Milford..." I accidentally uttered, then covered myself by saying, "Wiz mentioned something about going to Milford, is that where you're talking about Duane?"

Chiffon gave us a strange look, because a lie lingered in the air and the truth could be smelled from a distance. If she stared at Duane any harder his eyes would have confessed everything.

"How in the hell does she know where *my* man is goin' before I do?" Chiffon pulled Duane to the side, "what's goin' on baby, you're actin' funny what's up?"

"Nothin's up baby I gotta' go outta' town for a minute, I'll see you tonight okay? You know I gotta get dat paper."

As I hopped in the back of DR's Rover to supposedly get dropped off with Wiz, I waved bye to Chiffon from outside, but she didn't look too happy about me riding in the back of her man's truck without her in the front. Chiffon used to joke all the time on how her man was lactose intolerant, meaning that he couldn't stomach white girls, but as soon as Duane met me he came down with a little jungle fever.

Duane and I first met when I was staying at the Honeyspot Inn, a shitty motel outside of Bridgeport. We literally met by accident. I was driving Breeze's rental down Stratford Avenue one day, trying to roll a blunt and drive at the same time, when I slammed into the back of Duane's Beemer. Duane jumped out ready to kick my ass until noticing that I was a female, a fly one I might add.

Duane's nostrils flared as he bit down on his lip checking me out. He had a squint in his eye like *I'd love to get me some of that*, so I stepped out the car to let him feast his eyes on the rest of me. Duane moved back to let me out, licking his lips the whole time.

"Yo you okay?" He eventually asked.

"I should be asking you that question," I batted my eyes, "I'm sorry, I wasn't paying attention."

Duane didn't know that I knew Chiffon at the time, so he kept staring at my shear top, which exposed my huge pink areolas. My nipples were so hard they could have cut glass.

"Well it doesn't look that bad," I stated while bending over to look at the damage.

Given that I didn't have any panties on under

my short skirt, I knew Duane was peeking and getting aroused.

"*It doesn't look that bad?*" Duane scowled, "look at my shit!" "Those used to be custom LED tail lights now look at 'em!"

I got scared for a minute cause I thought he was going to report the accident. Breeze would have had a fit, especially since I didn't have my license yet.

"Don't worry about it," Duane said, "You're lucky you're cute. I'll have one of my mechanics fix it, but you should watch where you're goin' next time."

I knew Duane had long money, so I thought to myself, "*fuck Chiffon, this is my chance to bag a big time nigga... go for it bitch.*"

I gave a seductive smile as I walked circles around Duane in a flirtatious kind of way and said, "Well since I hit you from the back I guess I should return the favor and let you hit me from the back."

When I poked out my ass Duane became tantalized.

"Do you think you can handle it?" I whispered in his ear as I slowly traced my protruding nipples with my fingernail.

I caught him off guard, so it took Duane a minute to respond. He was speechless.

"You know what they say," he shifted his crotch, "once you go black you'll never go back."

"Nah I think it's more like once you go white you'll never be right."

"A lil' sexy thing like you might get whiplash fuckin' around wit' me. You sure you want your back blown out?"

"Yeah I like it ruff," I said, before tossing Duane my room key, "if you can beat me to the telly you can give me whiplash, dicklash or whatever else you wanna' beat me with."

Duane ran back to his car thrilled as hell. The challenge excited him even more. He floored it into a u-turn, while I was already passed the light headed for the entrance ramp. It was like we were in a cannonball run and sex was the prize. Breeze's Pontiac Rental car that I drove was no match for the *745I BMW* that Duane drove, so of course he won.

"What took you so long?" Duane laughed when I finally entered the room, "I got forty-five minutes so face down and ass up!"

His assertive manner made me hotter than a bowl of southern grits. He sucked my nipples through my thin shirt than stripped me down until I was ass naked.

"Wait a minute?" I complained on all fours acting as if I was a little schoolgirl, "can I please have a piece of candy first mister?"

"Sure, do you like Mr. Good Bars?" Duane played along, "it melts in your mouth not in your hand."

"Oh my god," I laughed in astonishment, "that thing's enormous!"

Duane stuffed the entire length of his monster down my throat and I didn't even gag. Over the years my mouth had become a regular sperm receptacle and he didn't know that I could drink a man better than Jenna Jameson. Duane loved it when I tried to talk while swallowing his huge cock, and take it from me, etiquette is not a factor when you're sucking dick.

The dirtier I talked the more turned on Duane became. He was trembling with ecstasy and I knew in twenty minutes after the award winning blowjob, Duane would be eating out of the palm of my hand or should I say, the crack of my ass. He ordered me to stop doing what I was doing then he placed my legs behind my head in a pretzel position.

It was as if my vagina was the Matrix as Duane went in and out in a slow motion manner switching his deep energetic strokes to hyper speed thrusts. Duane's long shaft and bulbous head felt like a meat missile exploding inside of me as he let out a loud manly moan.

"Aawwwww!" He sounded as he came all over chest.

"Damn you should've told me you were coming," I pouted, "I wanted to do my thing."

Duane looked at his chrome Tag Heuer watch then gasped with a relieving grin, "fifteen more minutes can't hurt, let me see what I can do," he said, as he left handedly stroked his penis.

I wasn't into any R. Kelly type shit, but I enjoyed being splashed in the face with spunk. Hot sperm made my skin clear. My sister Jenny used baby urine on her skin, but I'd rather have a sperm facial on mine. To each their own.

"Stop being silly," I laughed at how fast Duane jerked himself off, "I got you baby just lay back and let me work it."

First I massaged Duane all over his body to get the nerve endings circulating again and then I worked the middle with my long pierced tongue. In no time Duane's third leg was revived. After some more deep anal sex, I gave Duane the tug job of his life, until he gushed a happy ending all over my grill. Satisfaction guaranteed.

Following our first episode at the motel, I could've planted a flag on Duane's behind, cause that ass was mine now. He testified that I was the nastiest chick he had ever been with. Chiffon never took it in the face and by no means was she going to suck him off in between a nasty butt fucking. She was wifey, but I was Duane's very own porno star.

That's How I Do

When Duane found out how close Chiffon and I was he started to back off a little. I could not afford to stay at a motel any longer and given the fact that Duane had big chips, I convinced him to move me into an apartment on Capital Avenue. Duane paid for the first two months rent and security deposit to keep me quiet, but said I would have to pay my own rent from then on. He trusted me enough to stash some of his drugs in my apartment, which was fine with me, because I sniffed a little here and there whenever I wanted to. He had no idea the type of bitch I was. If he ever tried to play me I would backstab his ass when he least expected it.

After weeks of intensive scrutinizing, I finally discovered Duane's weakness and it wasn't daily head and good pussy. D-R was poor growing up, so now that he was paid, he wanted more than nothing to be accepted by white people as a successful black man. Rather than emulate their own rich and noble heritage, negroes like this imitate other races and think that in order to be truly successful, they have to have a White girl trophy on their arm. I am not complaining I'm just telling you like it is.

Instead of the usual routine of hanging out in the hood, I showed Duane what Fairfield County had to offer. I think he got off on the reaction people gave us when we walked in exclusive stores and restaurants arm and arm. After finding out that I was originally from Fairfield, Duane made me introduce him to all of my uppity friends from Laurelton Prep that we bumped into here and there. Most of their parents were political or prominent members of the community and in a few short months, Duane and I were "the couple" to invite to a party if it needed narcotic catering.

Before getting involved with me, Duane had most of his money invested in street sales, which was very profitable on its own. However I set up a more discrete drug trade on the academic and private party circuit that blew Duane's business up ten fold.

My links to the suburbs and colleges gave Duane the opportunity to expand his operation all over Connecticut and lock up the market. We set up stash houses in every dorm on every college campus in the area. Duane even hired mall security guards I knew to move product for him. The arrangement was simple. I would hand out the packages and Duane's lieutenant Wiz would collect the paper. Duane didn't have to touch nothing. His hands were clean. It was a win-win situation for him.

Seeing as we were making so much money off of my connections, I figured Duane would cut me in for more money, but when it came to giving up the cash Duane acted tight. Yeah he kept me looking good, pretty and all that, but no doe. Well he did buy a few designer dresses and a $7,000 Chinchilla fur once, but I felt like saying fuck all this bullshit, *gimmie the loot gimmie the loot!* I earned all that shit anyway.

If I had to estimate how much money I pulled in for Duane compared to myself, it would easily have been in the quarter to half a mill range. I deserved way more than the small allowance he gave me for all the shit I stored and carried for his ass, but fuck it. I enjoyed being his bitch at the time, so I kept my complaints to myself. I guess you get what you pay for.

In this game in order to stay on top, you need to be needed, so I made sure that I remained the middleman between Duane and our suburban clientele or I was going to be wearing rabbit fur instead of Chinchilla. On occasion Duane would have me drive to Harlem with one of his loyal soldiers to pick up Baggies. Not the kind of sandwich bags one would find in the supermarket, but the cellophane kind drug dealers use to identify their brand. If Duane had done business with the stores in Bridgeport that sold drug-packaging supplies, the cops would get an idea on how much product he was moving, so he did his thing out of town.

Duane's loyal solider at the time was this kid they called Burner. Duane named him that because Burner always bust his gun at Duane's command. My relationship with Burner was strictly business. I had no intention cheating on Duane with him at this point. For one, I made more money than Burner, which wasn't saying much, and two I really wanted to show Duane I was loyal.

Burner had just got out of jail not too long ago and he was cool to be around because he seemed to listen and respect my ideas. Duane didn't want to hear it when I told him he should invest in selling designer drugs. A true entrepreneur looks toward the future and the future was in pills.

After proving that he could keep his mouth shut, Burner and I started our own little thing on the side. It was nothing big, just a little something to pull in extra cake. We split everything fifty-fifty. Burner was the muscle and I was the manufacturer. In addition to selling weed laced with embalming fluid, I made Rophnol and Ecstasy suppositories for the suburban Rave parties. In this form, X lasted 2 to 3 hours longer than it did on sheets of paper. Club kids didn't have to worry anymore about getting caught with drugs in their pockets, when they could easily stick a suppository up their ass while they danced.

One day after we picked up the stuff for Duane, we hit the Bruckner expressway headed back to Bridgeport. I didn't think about Duane all day until I checked my messages. I was upset at the fact that he hadn't called me once to say hi or I miss you or whatever. Duane was probably with Chiffon or some other chick he kept on the side that I didn't know about.

I found out from one of my customers that Duane had two other jump offs around town. Just like he did for me, he also paid for their apartments cause they stored his drugs. I couldn't get mad at Duane, because I knew the game. There are valleys and peaks to the shit. At the end of the day it is all about business.

For most of the ride back to Connecticut, Burner stayed silent. There wasn't any bad energy between us, we were just high as hell enjoying the new mix CD's we copped off the 125th street bootleggers.

"Yo what are thinking about so hard over there" I asked Burner as I switched lanes with the smoothness.

"Nothing important," Burner held back a smile as he passed me the blunt.

"Stop lying," I said, "you keep looking over here like you wanna say something to me, what it is it?"

"I was just thinking 'bout how it would be on top of you," Burner came clean, "Ya boy ain't had none since he came home na'mean... all I do is hustle I never have any time for fun."

Burner's little crush on me was cute. I had to change the subject just to extinguish the sudden burst of horniness he caused me. I was really considering giving Burner some until I thought about Duane.

"*Maybe he's using Burner to test me,*" I wondered as I pulled into the McDonalds on the highway rest stop, "Maybe he wants to see if I would fuck with one of his subordinates?"

Out of the blue, Burner leaned over and kissed me. Before I could tell him to stop he kissed me again with his soft juicy lips. He held the back of my neck with his hand and added in a lot of wet tongue this time. I admit that I was smitten for the moment, but I came to my senses very quickly.

"If you want this bad enough you gotta' eat it first," I said while I hopped in the back seat.

Burner removed my FCUK sweats then pulled my cherry thong to side with his teeth. In no time a tongue slithered rapidly against my clit.

"*This boy is good,*" I said to myself as I died out the weed, "*I wish Duane would eat me out like this.*"

My moans increased as Burners tongue

pressure increased. I emitted a low cry and to my own surprise came all over Burner's face as I clamped my legs. Just as Burner began to unzip his jeans assuming that I would return the favor, a State Trooper knocked on the window with his flashlight. If the windows weren't all fogged up, the trooper would have seen me pull up my sweat pants.

"Is there a problem here ma'am?" The trooper asked as he leaned his head into the car on Burner's side.

"Not at all officer... I seemed to lose my contact lens," I smiled at him innocently, "I know how this might look, but my friend was helping me search for it back here."

The trooper got a call on his radio then frowned as he walked back to his cruiser. Burner and I laughed cause we thought he may have smelled the natural cunt odor on his face. If I had been a black chick smoking reefer and getting it on in the backseat, you best believe the trooper's response would have been more like *license and registration.*

I'm glad the State Trooper blew up the spot because I wasn't planning on returning the favor. It was a case of 68 and I owe you one.

Before we pulled off I called Duane on his Nextel.

"Yo where you at?" I chirped

"At the Barbershop, where the hell you been?" Duane chirped back.

"The city. Wait at the barbershop I'm coming by to see you," I clicked off.

Burner was mad because he realized that he wasn't getting any. I dropped Burner off on the block then met Duane at the Electric Hand Barbershop. We drove to my spot down the street to drop off the packaging supplies, but unfortunately there was someone waiting for us that I did not want to see.

"What does he want now?" I sighed, when noticing Manny's car parked in front of my apartment.

In or out of prison, Manny was still a fucking pest. On his second furlough he tracked me down for some ass and I regretfully broke him off a little piece. Two weeks after we had sex, I told Manny I was pregnant by him and needed money for an abortion. His gullible ass believed it, and gave me $400 that I think I used on a pair of shoes to wear to the club.

I kept Manny around as my run to guy, until I met Duane and witnessed how feared he was in the streets. Manny was terrible in bed and drove a throwback Maxima that everyone else called a hooptie. The only good thing I liked about Manny was that he was a total thug. Some chicks might not admit it, but every woman keeps a crazy nigga in their pocket for those times when they need beef settled or whatever. Other than that, Manny was worthless and now with Burner on my bra strap, I had enough goons in my life.

As we pulled to the curb I caught sight of the slightly jealous look on Duane's face. It was cute to see Duane jealous, so I kissed him on the lips and told him what the deal was.

"Is that your little boyfriend?" Duane inquired nonchalantly.

"Hell no! He's just some nobody I used to fuck wit' a long time ago," I said, "He won't leave me alone that's all. You know I got that good shit that keeps niggas coming back for more."

"I don't like the way this kid looking at us if he got a problem we can handle it right now," Duane said as he reached for his gun.

"Chill baby that's not necessary I'll be right

back," I said as I got out the car.

Manny stood by the entrance looking pissed. He mean mugged Duane from a distance trying to figure out who I had with me in the rental.

"Where da' hell you been at?" Manny yelled out, "I've been waiting out here for an hour already! I told you I was coming by to get my shit!"

"What shit!" I hollered back just as loud, "the four hundred dollars I beat you for? You're hit for that get outa here!"

Manny called me all kinds of bitches and hoes then flicked his cigarette at my back when I walked away from him. I rushed up the steps struggling with his tight grip on my arm, until Duane jumped out of the car to pull us apart.

"Jaz go upstairs and stop arguing wit' this clown," Duane commanded as Manny released his grip.

Duane was not as muscular as Manny, but he was still strong and in excellent shape. Manny lashed out at Duane like he was the hardest thing since Tony Montana.

"Yo get the fuck off me son," he yelled at Duane, "mind ya' fuckin' business before you get hurt son! Dis' between me and Jaz! Who you think you puttin' ya' hands on son?"

"I suggest you ease up before you find out!" Duane said before pushing Manny to the ground, "Jaz *is* my business..."

As soon as I came back outside Manny tried to act hard in front of me. He got up off the ground and rushed Duane like a football player. Unflustered with the athletic moves of a running back, Duane easily dodged the tackle. He then displayed a .357 Magnum, which stopped Manny dead in his tracks. Manny's face filled with trepidation and he backed away on all fours as Duane stood over him with the Magnum. Duane pistol-whipped Manny across the face three times, leaving him bloody and bruised on the cement walkway.

"And don't let me catch you 'round here no more or that's yo ass!"

"I'ight chill man, don't shoot!" Manny pleaded with dirty grass and blood falling from his mouth, "please man don't do it!"

"Baby that's enough, let's go," I said, while laughing at how stupid Manny looked crawling away.

For some reason violence excited me. I got off on the shit. Only in the hood could I experience such a thrill of two black men fighting over me.

"I'm glad you didn't blast him in front of my neighbors," I exhaled as we drove away, "the last thing I need is police asking me questions again."

"I'm glad you understand that," Duane looked me in the face, "from now on I don't want anybody at your crib except me you got that? Nobody!"

"But what happens if Manny tries to come back at me for what you did to him. What should I do then?"

"Trust me, he don't want nothin... I'm dat nigga you don't wanna fuck wit na'mean, C*all me Mister what's really good, I'm so hood, niggas know not to fuck wit D-R, I'm up to no good down for whateva, stackin' cheddah, packin chrome burners for slow learners, I got all types of tools for fools wit' silly problems, two shots from the three fif easily solves 'em...*"

Although I giggled at Duane's little rhyme, I didn't feel as confident as he did. I knew Manny would seek retribution.

Buck Fifty

He Loves Me Not

At first I was merely in search of a paid nigga with a platinum dick, but now I was starting to catch serious feelings for this cat. It wasn't so much about the money, as it was about where I stood compared to Chiffon.

"This shit ain't working out Duane I need more!" I bust out and said, as we rode in Duane's Escalade one day.

"More what money?" Duane asked.

"You know what I'm talkin' about Duane don't play dumb with me, I need more out of our entire relationship. You don't seem to have a problem parading me around the suburbs, but when we're in the hood you act like you're scared to be seen with me now. What's up with that?"

"Here we go," Duane sighed, "you must've been

watchin' Oprah again or some shit Dr. Phil co-signed."

"No fuck that! I'm tired of watching Chiffon treat you like a child. She's your ghetto princess and I'm your backseat mistress. All she does is spend your money. I don't even know why you're still with her stuck up ass?"

"Hold up Jaz, I make the money and you get the dick that's basically it with us. Chiffon's a real money earner not to mention my son's mother, so she could spend doe all damn day if she wants... that's what wifey does."

"I'm not a fucking money earner!" I shouted in outrage before throwing the three-inch thick knot of twenties I collected from my neighbor, "all I did was introduce you to cash. Fuck this shit! From now on do your own transactions!"

"What'chu want me to do Jaz, break up with Chiffon and make you my number one cause you introduced me to a few college kids?" Duane laughed, like the thought was absurd, "You got a fat ass and all that baby, but I ain't leaving Chiffon for no white chick. You crazy!"

Duane flipped through the money like it was a deck of cards then tried to hand it back.

"Fuck it then. If you don't want it I'll give the shit to someone else that does," he said after I pushed his hand away.

"You think I'm some bird bitch don't you?" I retorted, "My family is fucking rich I don't need you or your fucking money Duane! Just take me home I'm through with you."

Oh my god, I was fuming at the things Duane said about me. I didn't say a word for the entire ride back to Bridgeport now that I knew how he truly felt about us. This bastard tried to play me like I was Teena

Marie and he was Rick James. I almost slipped and called him the black ass nigger that he was, but I caught myself.

Losing me didn't only mean losing some good ass, it also meant losing a lot of customers. So after Duane thought about it more, he began kissing my ass.

"You still mad," Duane tapped me to break the silence, "you look adorable when you're mad, you know that?"

Duane made sexy eyes at me then said, "I can't leave Chiffon that easily. You don't understand it's deeper than our son."

He started rubbing my breast and feeling my leg while he drove. All Duane had to do was touch me and I forgot how mad I was. It was like he never said what he did.

"Who lives here?" I asked when we pulled up to this posh, although modest home on Lakeside Drive, "cause I'm not running no more packages for you today."

"Does this really look like a crack house?" Duane shook his head in amusement.

The house was small enough to keep the FEDS away, but the row of luxury vehicles parked in the drive way let the neighbors know what time it was. I could have melted in the seat when Duane told me it was his crib. Like a ten year old walking into Disney World I smiled ear to ear as we pulled into the garage.

"You said you never let nobody know where you rest your head, why you bringing me here now?" I questioned.

"Cause I felt like it," Duane affirmed, "Chiffon don't wear the pants I'm the fuckin' boss! This is my house!"

According to Duane I was the first chick that he ever brought to his home outside of his fiancé. He said that I should feel honored, because he would probably never do it again. I guess this was his way of making up for how he treated me earlier.

Duane carried me up to the bedroom as someone else in the house played 50 Cent's new joint at mid volume.

"*Hustle hard, money stack, sell that dope, sell that crack, sell that pack, sell that gat, sell that pussy, holla back! Hustle hard, money stack, sell that dope, sell that crack, sell that pack, sell that gat, sell that pussy, holla back.* "

"Yo that's my song turn that shit up," I bopped to the beat.

"Yeah whateva' just jump in the shower and I'll be back in a minute."

While Duane ran downstairs to get the phone, I curiously checked out every room upstairs. At the same time as Chiffon gossiped at her salon about other girl's men who were creeping, I was in Miss Bad Ass's bedroom standing stark naked skimming through her jewelry box. Before I got in the shower, I called the salon on my cell to make sure Chiffon was still there and not on her way home.

"*Chiffons glamour and gossip, Sandy speaking...*"

"Hi is Chiffon there?"

"Chiffon's with a client right now can I take a message?"

"No that's okay, I was just wondering if she had time to fit me in for a wash and set today?"

"Chiffon's gonna have her hands full for at least 4 more hours, would you like me to..."

All I needed to hear was 4 hours, and then I hung up in Sandy's face. That was more than enough time for Duane and I to stain the sheets. It was time to freshen up. As I washed all the right places someone slid open the shower door.

"Who the hell are you?" I screamed in shock as this stranger stood there looking at me.

"I'm Duane's lil' brother Terrell," he voiced softly, while gawking at my lathered body.

"Duane!" I persistently called out, "hey Duane you up here?"

"Chill baby D-R had to step out for a minute," Terrell gladly informed me, "when you got out the shower he told me to tell you that he'd be back in twenty minutes."

"Am I out of the shower yet? Obviously you don't listen!" I snapped, "do you like what you see Terrell?"

Terrell just shook his head yes, while grinning ear to ear as he looked me up and down.

"Good! Now close the door and go beat your dick in your own room!"

Terrell was aroused from what he saw obviously, because that horny smile on his face said it all. He was cute for his age I must admit and on any other day I would have pulled him in the shower with me and rode his skinny ass like a witch on a broomstick. But I figured why fuck a prince when you could fuck the king.

After rinsing off, I paraded around the bedroom in one of Chiffon's terry cloth robes. I spread out on her king-sized bed then lightly sprayed the satin sheets with a mist of my own perfume. Chiffon was going to go crazy when she found the strands of blonde hair I left on her pillow. She told me once that she thought her assistant had the hots for Duane, so I wrote Sandy's cell number on a piece of paper and slid it under the jewelry box to fuck with her head even more.

The next deceitful thing I did, hoping to stir up a little conflict, was smear a smidgen of lipstick on the fly of Duane's jeans that were balled up in the hamper. Lastly I tossed my draws under the bed and laughed my ass off. When I heard Duane pull into the garage, I hurried downstairs like I just got out the shower.

"*I swear yo, I can't stand Chiffon's pops! He thinks I'm his slave or some shit,*" I overheard Duane say with a belligerent attitude, "*he called me over his house just to move a goddamn couch! Can you believe that shit Rell.*"

It all started making sense to me why Duane kissed Chiffon's butt so much. Her father was a prominent Judge. Choosing to stay with her over me had nothing to do with beauty at all. Chiffon was his get out of jail free bitch. Her father knew exactly what Duane did for a living, but he was not going to let his grandson grow up with a daddy behind bars. Judge Davis kept Duane's drug dealing ass out of prison all these years, because his little girl fell in love with a hustler.

"Yo Rell, take this up to my bedroom then go play some video games," Duane instructed Terrell when I strolled into the kitchen. He undid my robe and offhandedly whispered sexual connotations.

I was his whore and he knew it. We fucked right there on the cold marble kitchen floor then did it again in the master bathroom. Two grams and couple of snorts later, Duane filled the tub up with a case of Louis Roederer that he made Terrell carry up from the pantry. Whenever Duane was fed up with Chiffon or her family I noticed he would always get drunk or carelessly waste money. It was his way of venting I suppose.

"Wouldn't this be fun if we could do this everyday?" I stated as Duane pulled on his cig, "Champagne baths and a nice long hard fuck on the daily can make a woman do crazy things ya' know. Chiffon better watch her back," I playfully threatened.

"That's how I feel about her father," Duane sounded stressed, "I hope that muthafucka' has a heart attack the next time he decides to move some furniture."

"I'm here for you baby," I spoke softly as I massaged Duane's tense shoulders, "forget about Chiffon and her father," I sucked my teeth, "she's a gimmick anyway, I'm the real deal and you know I'll do anything for you... you want me to kill 'em?"

"Stop buggin," Duane frowned, "I ain't saying all that."

Duane ended up drinking an entire bottle of Cris by his self. By now he was Bobby Brown drunk. He let his guard down and started talking about how much money he had where it was stashed. Duane didn't have to prove nothing to me, but his ego wouldn't let him stop bragging. After all this time I finally caught him slipping. I finally had the insurance I needed.

Duane even made a drunken promise to take me to the Funk Master Flex auto show in Hartford and you know I was going to hold him to it when he sobered up the next day if he fronted.

"But Chiffon told me that you were taking the family to the Yankee/Boston game that weekend? How you gonna pull this one off?" I wondered out loud.

"If I say we're going to the car show goddamn it! Then that's where we're going I said!"

While Duane went on and on about how much he hated Chiffon's father, I tuned him out and selfishly thought about myself. W*hat am I going to wear? What* *hairstyle should I rock?*

For the next five days our routine consisted of sniffing eight's, counting drug money and screwing in public places. I made sure Duane came at least two times, before I sent him home each night.

The Auto Show weekend ultimately came and I couldn't wait to go. All of the big dogs were going to be there, so I had to look hot. At the last minute I decided to strut my stuff in a $5000 silk Gucci cocktail dress that I bought in Beverly Hills, instead of wearing the run of the mill Dolce & Gabbana outfit that I borrowed from Chiffon's closet.

I can't begin to tell you how spicy I looked. The way that smooth silk clung to my curves made it obvious that I was wearing nothing underneath. My ass shook like Jell-O hello! Oh and my shoe game was sick. Free from *106 & Park* had nothing on me. Nobody could mess with the $2000 Australian gator knee high FMB (short for Fuck Me Boots) I wore that day.

Since Chiffon's Jewelry box was just sitting in the bedroom collecting dust, I assumed that she wouldn't miss any of her precious jewels. Her diamond choker looked splendid on me I must say. Duane bought Chiffon and I so much jewelry, he didn't even realize that I was wearing his fiancé's necklace.

When we got to the Civic Center it was off the chain. Duane left all the ghetto fabulous rides parked at home and more suitably drove us in his newly purchased Canary yellow Bentley.

The entire place was wall to wall packed with certified hustlers and auto lovers alike. We must have snapped pictures with like every rap star in the building. Though most of the rappers had wives or model looking chicks by their side, they still kept their eyes on yours truly and they weren't looking at my boots I can tell you that. I kept being mistaken for Ice T's wife. Even the hardcore pro-black MC's tried to holla' at me on the low. Just like the car owners exhibited shiny exotic vehicles, I displayed the new phenomenon of white girls with exotic booty. Duane never held his arm around my waist as much as he did that day. You couldn't tell me shit, except *you go!*

After the star-studded event, we got something to eat at Belly's Take-Out in Hartford. It was my idea to pick up some fast food, because I couldn't wait to show Duane a good time for showing me a good time. He wanted to get a room at the Honeyspot Inn for old times sake, but I pleaded that he take me to his house again for other reasons. I massaged his balls for most of the ride home, but never touched his massive hard-on not even once. I made Duane starve for my wetness as if he never hit it before. He practically begged me for head, but I wouldn't do that either.

I teased Duane so much so that his mushroom shaped dickhead turned purple and it throbbed uncontrollably. I couldn't wait to unleash its tension. So as soon as we pulled up to the crib it was on. The fact that I wasn't wearing any panties made it easy for Duane to lick me as I bent over the hood of his Bentley. Duane sipped and blew on my sensitive clitoris like a person drinking hot cocoa before he dug me out. He flipped me around then wrapped my hair around his hand as he pulled my head back like I was a horse and he was the jockey in charge.

My god, I'll never forget how good it felt to feel the heat from the car's engine against my back when Duane switched positions to slam it Mandingo style. I experienced waves of orgasmic sensations that only Duane could give. The garage door wasn't even closed yet and yet this man had my knees pressed to my chest fucking me like an epileptic on speed. If the neighbors across the street were watching us, they got to see one hell of a show.

Seconds after the hardest orgasm I had ever felt in my entire life dripped down my inner-thigh, the entire mood plummeted faster than a manhole cover falling off the Empire State Building.

"Oh shit!" I yelled out, "stop Duane, stop it!"

Duane thought stop meant, *keep going I want more*, but this time I really meant fucking stop.

"I CAN'T BELIEVE THIS SHIT!" yelled Chiffon as she stormed up the driveway with a clear view of Duane still inside of me, "OH HELL NO!" She said, "HELL FUCKIN NO!"

"Oh shit!" was Duane's first response, "It's a mistake baby let me explain!"

"Yeah right you tripped and slipped in her pussy by accident you lying bastard you," Chiffon screamed, "how could you do this to me! ...*WHAP!*"

She smacked Duane in the head with the mini Yankee bat in her hand. Chiffon's cousin Kim rushed the boys back into the Range Rover as Chiffon chased me around Duane's Escalade in a livid rage.

"My brother was right," Chiffon spat as I blocked her wild bat swings, "you ain't shit nothin' but a trick ass whore Jaz! ...*WHAP!*"

The next thing I know I was on the ground. Chiffon kept kicking and kicking, as I lay there curled up in a ball. Given that I didn't really know how to rumble yet, I didn't fight back and could only defend myself. The blows to my head ultimately knocked me unconscious.

"I just know she is not wearing my shit!" Chiffon uttered in disbelief, "I just know this white trash bitch ain't wearing my fuckin' birthday present Kim!"

Chiffon snatched her jewelry off my neck then started crying in anger as if she was grief-stricken. She also took my Prada bag, which contained all of the money I had to my name. She thought it was hers too, but it wasn't. Duane had just bought us the same exact one like he always did with everything.

Eventually Chiffon stopped jabbing me in the stomach. She was totally heartbroken and her anger seemed to turn into sadness.

"I hate you D-R, I fuckin' hate you! How could you? I'm three months and you go and do this!" Chiffon voiced out the window as she pulled off in an emotional fury, "it's over mutha'fucka'! You ain't never gonna see your sons!"

While I crawled from up under the truck thinking the worst was over, I had another thing coming. Duane outrageously beat my ass where Chiffon left off. He said it was my fault that his forthcoming marriage was ruined, like I put a gun to his head and made him screw me all them times.

"I love you Duane!" I wept at his feet like a two year old begging him to stop, "why are you doing this to me!" I cried, "Please Duane I love you!"

"Shut up bitch! I knew..." Duane paused his declaration as he began to slap me around, "we should've... *Wham*!" he punched me in the head, "...went to a hotel... *Bam!* Like I said... *Wham!* White bitches like you are more trouble than your worth... *Bam*!"

The last punch knocked me out cold. Duane then picked me up. He carried my limp body over to a pile of foul-smelling garbage bags on the curb and tossed me in it before jumping in his car to catch up to Chiffon.

When I came to, I felt like an actual piece of

trash. In no way did I ever expect Duane to do me like he did. Here I was beat up and busted with my ass hanging out of my torn Gucci dress and a shiner under my left eye, walking down Main Street half barefoot with one broken boot heel. My lip was split and handfuls of hair were ripped out of my head, so I looked like I had survived a plane crash.

When I finally got home I collapsed on the couch in a dejected frame of mind. My sense of worth was destroyed once again and to make matters worse I accidentally stepped in a large pile of dog shit that was hidden in the grass walkway near my building. My entire body was in complete agony. I just wanted to go to sleep and dream myself away.

Thicker Than Water

The next morning I awoke to the thumping sounds of my fed up landlord demanding that I open the door and give him the four-months rent that I owed. To his apprehension I changed the locks, so he couldn't get in or confiscate my things like he did to the other tenants that didn't pay on time. I just stared at myself in the mirror in a sort of trance like state, ignoring his countless legal threats. I couldn't pay him even if I wanted to, because Chiffon took my bag with all the money I had to my name. I figured carrying my valuables on my person would be much safer than leaving them in the apartment, just in case Manny kicked in my door looking for his $400.

Behind treating my black eye with ice and inspecting the black & blue marks all over my arms and stomach, I decided to call Manny as a last resort.

I don't know why? I just did it.

"Hello..." Manny's groggy voice answered, since I woke him up early that Sunday morning.

"Boo you still sleep?" I uttered shyly.

"Who dis'?" He asked.

"I'm sorry bay-bee," I fronted as if I really wanted him back, "I missed you... you still mad at me Man?"

"Jaz?" Manny questioned in shock, "what the hell you want?"

"Yeah it's me baby. I called to apologize for what happened boo boo. You were on my mind and I just want to let you know that I had nothing to do with what went down that day. I told that asshole you were my boyfriend, but he said if I didn't leave with him he'd kill me" I said, before crying crocodile tears over the phone "and you too! I was so'ooo scared."

"You can save all that shit for the next nigga," Manny sneered like he was about to hang up the phone.

"No wait! What can I do to prove to you that I ain't fucking with that son of a bitch no more?"

"If you really ain't have nothing to do wit' it like you said, then tell me where this dead man lives. I wanna' know where he rests his head."

"Well I don't know the address, but I know what the house looks like," I answered in reprieve, "if I take you there is that cool?"

"That's even better," Manny said, "be home around ten tonight. I'll pick you up and we gonna go pay this cat a visit."

After I hung up the phone I felt reassured that I would get my revenge some way or another. To Duane I was just some jump off with a fat ass and profitable drug connections, so why not add devious devil bitch to his outlook of who I was.

Regardless of how Manny planned on handling Duane, I didn't want to live in the hood no more. Most of my family had cut me off when they found out I only dated black dudes, so there was no turning to them for help. In their eyes I was nigger lover, but actually I had enough with black folks. I wished I still had the privileges of being a regular white girl, but wishing is for suckers.

I packed what I could for wherever I was going, but before I snuck out the building I had to figure out a way to stop by my brother's house first. He never got back to me about my share of the insurance money all this time. Chad and that insurance money was basically my only hope of skipping town with some doe in my pocket.

"*Tap Tap Tap,*" I lightly knocked on my neighbor's door.

"Who is it?" MS. Walker merrily answered.

"It's Jaz grandma," I answered back just as cheerful.

"Who?"

"Jasmine from next door," I had to speak up so she could hear me.

Naturally, Ms. Walker wasn't really my grandmother, but she was like a mother to everyone who lived in the building. Even though she was an old black woman from the south who at one time had to let the master's children suckle her breast instead of her own children, Ms. Walker treated me kind nonetheless. Getting up there in age Ms. Walker was losing her senses and was now unable to drive. Inconsiderate tenants would take advantage of her kindness and borrow her car to do whatever they wanted to do, but I was just going to drop by my brothers spot real quick then return her car as promised.

"Hey Ms. Walker, I was wondering if you needed anything from the store? And I also wanted to know if I can use your car for a minute?"

"Sure sweetie, just make sure you put some gas in the car and if it's not any trouble can you pick me up a new TV guide?" Ms. Walker asked, as if the favor was on me.

"No problem I'll be back in a few."

When I got to Chad's house in Trumbull, CT he was watering the lawn with one eye closed and a cigarette hanging from his lip. He smiled suspiciously as I parked Ms. Walker's 1979 Gremlin station wagon in his three car garage driveway.

"What happened to your face?" Chad frowned when I stepped out the car with a black eye and a LV scarf on my head.

"Honey is *that* your sister? Asked the woman who was kneeled down in the garden pulling up weeds.

"What's that shit supposed to mean Chad! You better check your bitch at the door," I retorted as he made his way over to greet me.

"Calm down. She's not used to nigger lovers," he laughed and snorted like a pig, "look at you Jasmine, you look like hell turned over! They kicked you in the ass and sent you home didn't they?"

"Fuck you Chad. What happened to the insurance money is the real question?"

"Huh?" Chad looked away still giggling to himself.

"What's up with the fucking money? It's been a long time and I need it. Why haven't you returned any of my calls?" I insisted he answer me.

"Um, look we need to talk about that," Chad heaved a sigh, "I um, I, hey guess what sis? I'm getting married!" He broke out with sudden joy, "Kelly wants to travel the Caribbean first and you have to see the ring I bought... *honey come show her your ring.*"

I walked away leaving him and Kelly standing there as he rambled off silly excuses about how and why he spent my money on her goddamn 10 carat solitaire.

Before driving off the premises never to return again, I drove Ms. Walker's Gremlin onto the lawn where I then floored the gas. The spinning tires destroyed Chad's detailed landscaping. I kept doing donuts all through the soggy lawn, which splattered mud all over the place. Chad and his stuck-up bitch were left looking like two stupid assholes with mud on their faces by the time I let up off the gas pedal.

"Con-grad-u-fuckin-lations!" I shouted out the window before speeding off the property, "I hope you both die on your honeymoon!"

I was mad as hell and really counted on that insurance money to hold me down for a couple of months. Ironically my closet stored over $30,000 worth of shoes and clothes in it that I couldn't return or pack, and my cell phone bill was in the hundreds about to be turned off. Besides that I had a rising drug habit from doing recreational lines with Duane at house parties. Cocaine had become my run-to drug. With Duane I sniffed and smoked for free, but those days were done.

Tears streamed from my contact-less blue eyes as I sat waiting at a light. Instead of returning Ms. Walker's car like I promised, I swung by the projects and copped some blow with the last bit of change in my pocket. As I held the folded dollar bill with powder in it, I thought long and hard before sniffing.

"I know you're not going to' let one good ass

whooping chase you away?" A voice popped into my head, "*you know where Duane's stash is... you should rob his ass for what he did. You deserve it Jaz.*"

The idea sounded good at the time, so I thought out a plan and resumed sniffing.

Goodnight Kiss

When Manny picked me up I was so freaking wired off cocaine, it felt like my eyes were taped open. Even though it was dark as hell outside I wore a leopard print scarf and some big ass Chanel shades to cover my bruised face. As I attempted to throw my bag of clothes in the back, two cats with big guns on their laps greeted me uncouthly.

"Hurry up trick! Get your pale ass in the car before you let out all the smoke," one of them uttered, "and throw that shit in the front."

"You didn't tell me you were bringing people with us baby?"

"Never mind them just get in the car!" Manny grumbled.

Manny glanced at my peculiar garb and shook his head in reproach. He snatched off my shades then he tilted my chin to examine my face.

"He did you good didn't he?" Manny said after seeing the bruises, "just show me where the house is," he shoved my face away in disgust.

When we finally found Duane's house no one was home. Oddly enough there were no cars in the driveway and all of the lights were off. Chiffon was probably staying at her father's house, so we waited to see if Duane would show up. An hour later the security gate to D-R's driveway opened. Duane pulled through slowly in his Bentley. The dudes in the backseat hopped out quietly before the iron gate closed.

As Duane drunkenly wobbled out of the car, Manny and his crew jogged up the driveway with pistols dangling from their hands. Duane was too bent to see them coming. I got out the car duplicating their sneaky steps and by the time I made it to the garage, Manny and his boys had already had D-R spread out on the hood of his ride like they were the police making an arrest.

"If you don't stop squirming you're gonna get it right here!" Threatened the tall one with dreads, before he pistol-whipped Duane in the back of the head.

"Take his punk ass in the house," Manny ordered.

Duane was insensible. Manny sat on the couch aiming his .45 at Duane's head just in case he came to all of a sudden. The other two dudes and I ransacked the house looking for anything of value. Unlike them I knew what I was looking for and headed straight for the bedroom.

There was a pair of diamond stick earrings in Chiffons jewelry box that I just had to have. I tried them on the first time I was in the house and they looked splendid on me. So while going through her shit I stumbled upon a giant pink V.V.S cut diamond ring that had to be a fortune by itself. It was still in the box and a tiny card was taped to it. The note read: *Baby I do love you and I am truly sorry. Can you forgive me? There is no one else in the world for me.*

My eyes widened. It was a Kobe Bryant make-up ring, but Chiffon would never see it now.

The day Duane and I got drunk in the tub, he slipped up and told me where some of his money was stashed. He said he had a safe in the house, but didn't say where. All I knew was that he hid some of his re-up money in the bottom dresser drawer in the master bedroom.

"Yo y'all find anything?" Manny yelled from downstairs.

"Nah I found a couple ounces of weed, but no doe yet," one of his boys hollered back.

"How 'bout you Jaz?" Manny questioned loudly, "anything?"

I didn't know what to say as I stood in front of what looked like a million dollars.

"Nope!" I yelled, while stuffing my pockets with as many rubber banded knots that I could.

Seconds after padding my bra with a couple of grams of coke, Manny's two associates rushed into the bedroom with merriment on their faces when they seen all the loot still in the dresser.

"Oh shit! We're RE'OTCH BE'OTCH!" The short one with gold fronts yelled, imitating the David Chappelle voice as he rudely pushed me out the way.

One of them held open an empty pillowcase, while the other dumped the entire drawer of cash into it. They might have noticed the lumps in my pocket, but I don't think they cared. We all scurried downstairs where Duane was conscious again. Manny had him strapped to a lazy boy with duct tape around his face and chest. I peeled the tape from Duane's mouth to hear what he was trying to say.

"All you muthafuckas are dead!" Duane proclaimed, "especially you Jaz," he threatened before spitting at me, "Dead! Ya heard! Dead!"

Manny's boys took turns slapping Duane around. After busting him in the mouth with a bar stool, Manny pulled out his gat.

"What am I supposed to do with this?" I asked naively as Manny handed me his gun.

All the while I knew what he wanted me to do.

"What'chu think?" Manny plopped back down on the couch, "pop his ass and prove to me that you hate this nigga like you said on the phone. Don't you wanna make me happy?"

I wanted to say "no stupid, I'm just using your dumb ass" but I didn't.

Duane could barley talk with his mouth split open now, but amazingly he still kept mumbling shit about what he was going to do if he got free. I stood in front of Duane trembling. Manny lifted the barrel to Duane's head for me with his finger. I don't know why, but stabbing my father in the back was much easier for some reason? Even though I wanted to get back at Duane for beating my ass and humiliating me, I really did love him.

Manny and his crew turned up the pressure by cheering me on to squeeze the trigger.

"Do it! Do it!" They all yelled as if I was in college chugging down a beer, "Do that shit! Go! Go! Go! Go!"

I closed my eyes and tried to fire, but nothing happened. I squeezed it again and still nothing. Everyone laughed feverishly as the joke was obviously on me. My heart was pounding and I even had sweat on my brow. Manny had given me an empty gun and just wanted to see if I would pull the trigger.

"Yo you owe me a dub," Manny shouted to his boy, "I told you that bitch got it in her... I seen the killer in her cold blue eyes."

I was pissed. My back was soaked with perspiration and my hands were still shaking. I think if there had actually been bullets in that gun, I would've just shot Manny and his friends then bounced.

"BLOOM! BLOOM!" Two shots unexpectedly fired.

Without warning the dude with the dreads shot Duane in the chest at point blank range. The other one with the gold teeth snatched the empty gun from me and then slapped me on my butt with it as he pushed me to the door.

"How much you think we got?" Manny asked all excited.

"A lot nigga, just keep driving," Dread answered as if he was in control the whole time.

It was evident that Manny's two so-called friends didn't respect him and it made me real nervous. They kept looking at me whispering to each other in the backseat. Something didn't feel right. I had a bad premonition about these two.

"Yo Manny, pull over right here," Dread uttered as we passed a dark alley downtown.

"For what?" Manny answered hot and bothered.

"Man just pull over, I gotta take a piss," he complained.

When Manny pulled over Dread got out, while his boy stayed seated in the back. I was extremely tense with my hand on the door handle the entire time. No sooner than I turned around to look in the backseat a gun was pointed to my head.

"Click, Click."

I thought I was a goner, but the gun didn't fire. That stupid bastard tried to kill me with the same empty gun he took away from me back at Duane's house. He struggled to switch guns, but by the time he did I was out of the car running.

"Boom! Boom! Boom!" Dread fired three shots into Manny's head from outside of the car.

"Get that bitch!" He yelled.

I was already halfway down the street before they even realized it. Even though I felt a strong burning sensation in my back and stomach, I kept on running until I saw crowds of people. Who knew I could run so fast. When I hit the corner I dashed into Dunkin' Donuts and collapsed on the floor. Customers screamed when they seen all the blood on my shirt. Some of them even came over to help me, if you call taking everything out of my pockets help. They stole everything from me, including Chiffon's jewelry around my neck, wrist and fingers, plus the doe.

Five minutes later the ambulance came and I was rushed to St. Vincent's Hospital. My clothes were cut off of my body with huge scissors as the nurses checked for more bullet holes. When I awoke hours later, a young female doctor greeted me. My body was still aching from Duane and Chiffon's beat down and now it felt like a truck had ran me over. To top it all off the fucking police had cuffed me to the bedrail. I struggled to get free for a minute then sunk back into the bed out of breath.

"I have some good news and some bad news for you," the pencil neck doctor stated in her East Indian accent.

She took my blood pressure then wrote something on her chart.

“Oh really? What?” I asked in total agony.

“The good news is that you’re going to live. Your body is still in shock and you’ll be sore for weeks to come of course, but you’re going to make it. The bullet exited the side of your abdomen and tore a few vital organs, but we took care of the damage.”

I was glad, but the sorrowful look on the doctor’s face puzzled me.

“The bad news is... there was nothing we could do I’m so sorry you lost the baby.”

“What baby?” I started sobbing.

“You didn’t know that you were two and a half months pregnant?” The doctor asked oddly, “It looks like your body went into shock causing terminal stress on the fetus.”

I couldn’t stop crying. No one else but God knew how much I wanted to have a baby one day, but I didn’t even know I was carrying. All those times I threw up in the morning I just thought it was from a bad hangover from the night before and I never considered the cause being morning sickness. With all the raw dog sex we had, it had to be Duane’s.

“I really am sorry,” said the doctor, “but I have some more bad news. There’s an officer in the hall ready to take you into custody as soon as your I.V is complete.”

“For what!” I yelled at her, “I’m the one that got shot bitch! I just lost my fucking baby!” I screamed uncontrollably trying to kick at her while cuffed to the bed.

“Please calm down ma’am I’m just doing my job. If you cooperate I can see that you stay here tonight instead of going to jail. It’s procedure to notify the police of any type of shooting. Illegal drugs were found on your person, so there’s not much I can do if you scream and yell."

At the time I didn't know it, but a nurse in the emergency room had found the envelopes of coke in my bra when they cut my clothes off.

"That's Bullshit! I'll slap that red dot off your head if you don't un-cuff me right now!" I yelled.

"Officers," the doctor scowled as the two cops entered the room, "take it up with them... can you remove this woman at once please."

Any other girl would have flipped out too, if she had just lost a life growing inside of her that she knew nothing about and never mind the fact of not having a damn thing to her name when at one point she had it all.

I regretted taking things out on the doctor, because she was just trying to help me out. The price of my outrage was going to jail wounded and stressed. On the ride down to the Bridgeport police station, I made myself feel grateful by stressing the thought that I at least escaped death and would hopefully escape a murder charge for the second time.

I used my only phone call to call my brother Chad to see if he would bail me out, but the fucking answering machine came on.

"*You have reached Chad and Kelly we're not home right now...*"

"UUUUGGGHHH!" I sighed in irritation.

I was so frustrated that the police had to stop me from repeatedly slamming the phone against the cell wall.

The next morning I felt even more pitiful at the arraignment, because my bond was only $1000, which meant I only had to come up with 10% and I didn't even have that. All my money was gone and I was going to have to stay in jail until my next court date.

Since females were not allowed to stay in the North Avenue county jail for long, I was expecting to be shipped upstate to Niantic, which was the moment I feared.

Payback's A Bitch

The more things change, the more they stay the same. Kayla couldn't seem to escape violence either, so she embraced it. She drove through Brooklyn itching to fuck somebody up after receiving news that a friend was sent to the hospital. It didn't take long before Kayla spotted the person she was looking for.

"Is that that sorry excuse of a man?" Kayla uttered as she hit the brakes, before circling down Junis Ave.

"Yeah that's Millz," Sade confirmed, "he used to pump weed out'a Bristol Park, but now he moved up to crack. He's a real asshole. My brother used to sell for him."

"We should get his ass right now for what he did to Toya," Kayla exploded with bitterness, "this is the fifth time he sent her to emergency over some bullshit. You think he's holding heat?" Kayla asked.

"More than likely," Sade answered, "I know he's got mad beef wit' niggas, so he's probably strapped."

As they watched Millz step out of his Lexus coupe, Kayla inserted a clip into her 9mm before she got out the car. Kayla's usual weapon of choice, her fathers' straight razor, would have to sit this one out today.

The dude about to get it dated Kayla's close friend Toya. Toya was a member of Kayla's crew called the Buck Fifty Bitches, due to the 150 stitches they usually left on people's faces with their box cutters.

Toya's boyfriend Millz used to play ball overseas, but after breaking his ankle on the court he resorted to pushing crack when he returned to the States. Millz was very possessive and beat Toya's ass whenever he felt like it. He slapped her around for just about anything and this time he put Toya in the hospital with a broken jaw after noticing an unfamiliar number on her cell, which happened to be Kayla calling to say what's up.

Millz disappeared into his apartment building then came back out ten minutes later carrying a small travel bag. His long white T-shirt fit more like a skirt and from the protrusion around his waist it was obvious that he was indeed strapped. Kayla sat on the trunk of his car like she owned the shit. The streetlights beamed a glare off of her shiny black thighs, which captured Millz attention for a minute. It was as if Kayla heard his sexual thoughts. The squint in her eye revealed extreme dislike and when Millz got closer he tried to match Kayla's ice grill.

"Do I know you?" Millz hollered like he didn't appreciate Kayla all up on his Benz.

Kayla just shrugged her shoulders as she licked

her lollypop with little concern. Although Millz was up in her face talking shit, she just ignored him and kept conversing on her cell.

"I know you hear me talking to you bitch" Millz sneered, "get off my shit right now!"

"S'cuse me? What'chu just say?" Kayla tossed her lollypop to the side.

Before Millz could yank Kayla off his car, Sade crept up from behind and slapped him in the face with a tire iron. Kayla grabbed Millz around the waist quickly removing his gun, and then she karate kicked him in the back. The forceful punt caused Millz' head to hit the front bumper of the car parked behind his, before he fell backwards on the curb.

"Lay down and stay down!" Kayla yelled while she held Millz own gun to his ribs.

She then placed her cell phone to his ear to relay a cordial message from Toya.

"Fruuggkk yoouuggh Mrrillss" Toya muddled through the phone.

Being that Toya's mouth was wired shut, her words came out garbled, but Millz still recognized the voice and his face just dropped in regret.

"Smile for the camera asshole... *POW*!" Kayla shot him once in the kneecap, "that's for Toya and this is for calling me a bitch!" Kayla said, as she left the Buck Fifty trademark down the side of Millz cheek.

Millz screamed like a coyote in excruciating pain. Kayla and Sade fucked him up real good. No more triple doubles on the court for Millz, he probably wouldn't even be able to walk straight again.

"Now this one's for the hell of it," Sade bellowed before smacking him with the tire iron once more... *PLUNK*!

The last blow was solid. It smashed Millz jaw

like a piece of glass. Kayla used her videophone to transmit the whole thing directly to Toya's cell, while she laid in the emergency room. An eye for an eye or rather a jaw for a jaw made this one even as they left Millz squirming in the gutter.

On the way to visit Toya, Kayla dropped by Sade's sister's house to give her a ride to work. Sade's sister Michelle was a RN who worked at the hospital where Toya was admitted. As they walked through the doors that led to Triage, laughter could be heard. When Kayla pulled back the curtain she was greeted by Riva and Jackie, two other members from her click that she hadn't seen in awhile.

"What's really good wit'chu?" Riva addressed Kayla, "Damn Kay you got thick as hell girl what'chu been eating'?"

Seconds later a wrinkled old nurse threatened to have them all removed because it got so loud up in there.

"This is a hospital not a nightclub," the woman said, "if you can't keep it down I will have you all removed!"

They ignored the crabby nurse and exchanged hugs like old friends do. After fifteen minutes of reminiscing it was time to go.

"We just stopped by to see how you were doing," Sade said while giving Toya a hug goodbye, "Shell told me that she'll see you on her break."

Toya thanked Kayla and Sade for getting back at Millz before the nurse walked in with the security guard.

"So what do y'all bitches be doin' these days?" Riva jealously inquired as they walked out the hospital, "you got all fancy on us all of a sudden... wrist blingin' and shit? Drivin' new whips every month I heard. When you gonna put us on?" Riva waited for an answer.

"Yeah those rocks look sick" Jackie examined Kayla's wrist, "what's that about 5 carats?"

"I got somewhere to go but I'll tell you what," Kayla let Jackie stare, "meet us at my uncle's crib tomorrow night around eight. I have a proposition for you if you're interested."

The next night, 8:00 came around. Even though she was in excruciating pain, Toya, Riva, Jackie and the twins Nika and Mika, congregated outside of Johnny Red's house on Sutter Ave, until Kayla and Sade pulled up in a brand new gleaming Hummer.

Jealousy filled Riva's eye, but she played it off and smiled like the rest of her friends. Sade had on a sexy white lace bustier under a black leather motorcycle vest with skin tight Jeans. Kayla walked around from the driver side in a pair of leather shorts that complemented her heart shaped behind. Her full cupped breasts slightly moved side to side in the spaghetti strap top she wore as she made her way to the gate.

"I'm glad you all made it," Kayla said as she slid Jackie into a teasing headlock, "here's the deal. All of you knew my boyfriend Laquan and the things he used to do. Who could forget all them shootouts, but I got a way for us to get paid the same way he did... matter of fact better."

"Doin' what?" Jackie asked, "God knows I'm tired of gettin' followed around the stores while Riva boosts us something to wear to the club."

Riva kicked the back of Jackie's foot as they entered Johnny Reds house. She felt Jackie always gave too much information when she talked.

"Basically we're retiring anyone who gets on the shit list!" Kayla answered, "You know, like the drug dealers that sell crack to pregnant school girls and shoot little kids over short packages."

"And if you think it's all about the money you're wrong. It's about getting people back for the things they do," Sade added, "what we take we put back into the hood. I would like my children to have a chance."

"Get the fuck outta' here," Riva retorted sucking her teeth, "you pulled up in a brand new Hummer and we pulled up on the fuckin' D train! I don't know 'bout yall," Riva scanned the other girl's faces, "but I wanna' get paid. Fuck dat' righteous shit!"

"Chill Riva just listen first before you start runnin' off at the mouth," Sade angrily replied.

"Yeah bitch zip it! Listen to what the fuck she gotta' say before you start complaining," one of the twins intervened, "they're tryna' put us on, so shut the fuck up! Go ahead Kayla finish what you were saying."

"Don't get it twisted, there's rules to this shit and my heart is in this so watch yourself Riva. Nobody was there for us when we were running the streets slicing chicks over boys and gossip? All we got to show for it is scars and court cases, don't you wanna' step ya' game up? I know all about your lil' credit card scams and rip offs girl, we grown ass women now c'mon."

"Where exactly does the money go?" The other twin Nika asked, "and what makes you think we can't go to jail or get killed?" Her sister joined in.

"As far as the money is concerned," Sade replied, "some of it goes to a good cause and since a sista' gotta' look good, alot of it goes in our pocket. But there are plenty of organizations in the hood that really need the funds like this one program that helps children stay in touch with their parents or family members when they're locked up," Sade said, "it doesn't let prison sever families like it's intended to do. I know there's much more that could be done, but for now it's at least a start."

"And to answer your question Mika I can only promise you loyalty. I can't promise you that you won't get killed or go to jail," Kayla cracked her knuckles, "that's the risk you have to take to get what you want, but my uncle Red can train you to be the deadliest chick with a gun that the streets has ever seen."

"What's up Red, these are my girls Jackie, Riva, Toya, Mika and Nika and you already know Sade," Kayla announced as Red rolled into the room, "I brought all the stuff like you asked."

Johnny Red kept a straight face as he examined the girls from head to toe.

"Some of history's most brilliant warriors were women did you know that? But you girls look like softies to me," he said.

"Looks can bee deceiving," Riva simpered, before Red rolled back across the room.

Johnny Red was in a wheel chair after his legs were blown off in the war, but he was still the best combat and weapons trainer around. If you ever needed a weapon Johnny Red was the man to see. Kayla spread out a wool army blanket containing the latest handguns on the market. Each Glock looked brand new and the chrome weapons shined like Canal street silver.

"Ooh I like this one!" Nika grinned, while examining the Magnum in her hand.

"Not so fast," Johnny Red yelled out as he took the gun away from Nika, "these aren't toys or box cutters... those are yours over there."

Red pointed to a dirty duffle bag filled to the top

with guns that looked like they hadn't been used in years.

"What's this shit?" Riva complained, "I just got my nails done, come on Kayla we ain't come here to clean no dirty ass guns!"

"Shovel the shit somewhere else," Red chastised, "soldiers need to learn how to clean their own weapons. Back in Nam I-"

"We ain't in Nam nigga" Riva cut him off disrespectfully, "we in Brooklyn."

"You girls are gonna have to learn some discipline! Nothing in this world is for free! After you clean these old guns I'll give you the new ones. If that means breaking every goddamn nail on your fingers then that's what it means. Now get to work or get to steppin'!"

Riva sucked her teeth, but did as Red instructed. It took about a week to clean all of Johnny Red's weapons in his approved manner, but by the time the girls were finished, they could dismantle and assemble any gun in their sleep. Red's intentions were for the girls to discipline themselves and it started to work.

After a few more weeks of learning combat firing maneuvers and undergoing numerous loyalty tests, Kayla called for another meeting. She asked the girls to form a circle, then had them place each of their middle fingers above a large candle flame, before she pulled out seven rings from her pink Coach bag. Kayla then gently sliced their fingers, including her own, with a razor one by one.

When she got to Riva she stopped. Riva backed out. She thought the ritual was weird. Kayla just continued on as if Riva wasn't even there.

"As your blood drips into the fire so shall your soul burn in hell forever if you ever betray or snitch on any one of us, your friends. As your rings cover your wound so shall the power of the almighty cover and protect us. We form this bond for life and once you accept this there's no turning back," Kayla made clear as she watched each person's reaction, "that means never deceive anyone in this circle or take from anybody in the streets that don't deserve it. If you break these rules that's your ass! And I mean it."

After the ceremony Kayla passed out five more jewelry boxes that contained initialized BFB diamond bracelets inside. Everyone seemed excited except Riva. Riva felt that if she was going to rob and kill people why not keep 100% of everything. Riva wasn't one for sisterhood, but those diamond bracelets were swaying her opinion.

"*Who the fuck does Kayla think she is Oprah*?" Riva thought to herself with a smug look on her face, "*they got rules and I got rules too; fuck everybody else and do you!*"

"You in or out?" Sade put Riva on the spot, as she sat there looking up at the ceiling.

"I don't know yet, can you give me some time to think about this?" Riva asked with no intention of abiding by any set of laws or making new friends.

"We'll have to decide as a group," Kayla retracted the box sitting in front of Riva. She then turned her attention to the other girls, "...from this point on we all work as one."

While the rest of the crew tried on their new bracelets and talked, Riva bit into her honey bun looking disjointed as she thought about her opposing decision.

Weeks later it was on. Someone new was on Kayla's shit list.

"You ready?" Kayla whispered to her crew at the

stroke of midnight.

"As much as we're gonna' be" Sade responded before concealing her identity with a mask.

Kayla, Sade and Jackie entered an apartment hallway where a brand of dope stamped 'New York's Finest' was sold. Toya and the twins guarded the door from outside. *New York's Finest* was some powerful dope, even more potent than China White or Tango & Cash. Fiends were dying all over BK from it, which made it sell all the more. Kayla and Sade found the spot by following Millz one day.

"It's amazing how someone would want to buy some drugs that they know can kill them on the spot. Where's the fun in that?" Kayla thought to her self, *"Whoever's pushin' it needs a taste of their own medicine."*

The ski masks on the girl's faces and assault weapons in their grips caused the dope fiends waiting in line to cop, to scurry like rats. The girls kicked in the door like stick up kids with a vengeance, shooting shit up until no more shots were fired back at them. Kayla thought they were robbing the people Millz worked for, but little did she know that they would be going up against the boys in blue AKA New York's Finest.

As for the two addicts that stood behind the riddled door, their morning heartaches were now over. Bulletproof vests didn't help out much for the dealers guarding the front room either, because both girls packed AR-15's with 3 extra sets of clips containing hollow tipped rounds. When the dope powdered smoke cleared Sade looked surprised.

"Oh shit!" She said, "Look! They're fuckin' cops!"

Unexpectedly two police lieutenants still in uniform were caught in the middle of counting their weekly profits. Now they lay there dead on top of the cash. Pasta bowls and dope were scattered all over the kitchen table. The apartment was basically vacant except for drug packaging materials, a 13-inch Television set, a couch and kitchen cabinets that stored pounds of dope and tons of cash. Between the three of them, Kayla, Sade and Jackie had unintentionally eliminated a small team of crooked cops that were moving serious heroin throughout Brooklyn.

While Jackie and Kayla stuffed cinderblocks of cash in large duffle bags, Sade dumped the drugs in the sink and filled it with water. There was so much money lying around, that Kayla had to call Toya and Mika for help. With more than $200,000 in singles, fives, and tens, they fled the building unscathed as the fiends ran for their lives.

Buck Fifty

Time

Riva left things up in the air. She was 'doing her', so she never got back to Kayla and the rest of the girls about her final decision. Riva was up to her old ways again, despite Jackie's advice to leave the petty boosting alone and get down with some real money making schemes. Like any other girl into stealing garments for a living, Riva scoured the Tri-State in search of new malls to hit. This time she chose Stamford Town Center Mall in Connecticut.

Riva along with some other dumb bitch had fled all the way to the Stamford train station with thousands of dollars in stolen clothing items. The security team from Saks Fifth Avenue chased them out the Mall, but lost them in the rush hour crowds. A Good Samaritan joined in the pursuit and fingered Riva as she ducked behind commuters waiting for the train. The other girl wasn't that dumb I guess because she got away, but Riva got knocked. She struggled with the Metro police officers until a box cutter fell out of her bag.

"Don't move!" Officers closed in on her, "drop the weapon or we'll shoot!"

Riva was finished. Being that she had a blade and fought back scratching and kicking, the police trumped up the charges to assault with a deadly weapon on top of the grand larceny charges she faced. In a little while Riva would meet yours truly, known for the time being as inmate number 407112.

I never thought the day would come when I would be glad to be in prison, but doing time upstate was much better than sleeping in filthy ass county jail. This was my sixth month in the Niantic Correctional Institution and my last days were finally approaching. I only had 1368 hours left to go and I couldn't wait to get the fuck out of there. I think I could've beat those bullshit drug charges, but my public defender, or should I say public pretender, convinced me that I would lose if I fought the case, so I copped out to a possession charge. If I had money for a real liar, I mean lawyer, I know I could've just got probation.

"Yo white girl," an unfamiliar face shouted as I walked passed a table of chicks playing cards, "yo I'm talkin' to you snow white... you wanna' play spades or you too good to play with us?"

I looked around like I know she isn't talking to me, because nobody ever asked me to play anything with them.

"What are you deaf?" Riva tugged on my shirt, "I don't see no other white girls walkin' 'round here you wanna' play or what?"

During the entire five months in prison I hadn't talked to anyone except the C.O's. Everybody in there thought I was strange and usually left me alone because I talked to myself out loud. For some reason Riva acted different.

"Okay I'll play," I said.

Whenever it rained my bullet wounds would ache, so I sat down holding my side.

"Grab a seat cabrona," these two Puerto Rican girls laughed with each other.

"Let's see if it's funny when we set your asses" Riva spoke up in my defense.

Riva didn't look like she belonged in prison until she opened her mouth. She was a real feisty one. However her appearance was still totally feminine. She looked a lot like Christina Milian, just a little darker and much more thugged out. It was obvious by the way she talked that Riva was a hard rock. When she stood her legs arched back in such a sexy way, I thought was very appealing. Riva bragged that she was down for 10 months already and had two months left like me, but she seemed like she liked being in prison.

"So where you from," I began the conversation as Riva dealt out the cards, "you from Bridgeport?"

"Hell no I'm from Buck town baby, Brooklyn! Home of the original gun clappers if you don't know, but I got people in BPT" Riva said, before raising her voice to slam down an ace of spade, "I got knocked on some ole' larceny bullshit in Stamford, but the muthafucka's hit me wit' a weapons charge for havin' a box cutter on me can you believe that shit!"

After winning two games straight, Riva and I hit the showers before count time. Even though we shared the same cube, we had never really spoke until now.

While Riva closed her eyes to block out the soap, the water bounced off of her perky breasts. I watched the bubbles follow each curve down to the back of her leg. I scanned her heavenly body from head to toe before rubbing my box in a circular motion, fantasizing us in a 69.

Riva was beautiful point blank. I wanted her bad. Losing the baby and thinking about how Duane shit on me fucked up my head. Dick was no longer the highlight of my life. I don't know if it was from psychological trauma or what, but my attraction for men had gradually started to fade. I now found women more appealing, but I admit that I still craved a good dick every now and then.

When Riva noticed what I was doing she looked at me with a puckered smile. Those tantalizing lips of hers drove me wild.

"Damn girl you got some big ass knockers," Riva smiled again, "are they yours?" She asked, while wrapping a towel around herself.

"I guess so I paid for 'em right?" I returned the same enticing gaze, "go ahead you can squeeze 'em if you want to Riva don't be scurred" we both giggled.

Just as Riva was about to tweak my nipples, in walked two disgusting gargantuan looking bitches. Self-conscious about how it looked I guess Riva rushed back to the sink. I finished drying off as the fat Kirsty Alley looking heifers surrounded me.

"How much did these shits cost?" The ugliest one out of the two asked, as she grabbed my breasts really hard, "they feel like Nerf balls and shit."

"Get your fat hands off me," I pulled away backing into Riva, who was now brushing her hair in the mirror.

Everyday these same two whales tried to take

my food at lunch. If I didn't give it to them they stuck boogers in it so I wouldn't eat it. This time one of them had a disposable razor in her hand. The other stood there looking me up and down as she lit a cigarette from the arc of the light bulb socket.

See in prison bitches fuck with you when they find out you're about to go home. They figure they could do anything to you and you won't fight back, because you might jeopardize your freedom if you catch a ticket. Given that Riva was discharging, that theory didn't apply to her. Without any delay Riva turned around and smacked girl one with a sock full of AA batteries that she had hidden under her towel. Riva kept hitting the girl until she saw blood. Girl two seen her friend fall to the floor and took off running like a punk.

"Kick that hoe in her muthafuckin' head," Riva commanded as I stomped the bitch's face in.

Just as I got into kicking her ass, "RECALL, RECALL FOR COUNT," sounded over the loud speaker.

"Where I'm from we leave our trademark on bitches, go ahead cut her face," Riva handed me the girls blade.

"Yo a C.O's comin' lets be out," Riva stopped me from going off after I sliced the chick more than once.

We both hurried to our cube while fatso lay on the shower floor holding her cheeks. They never messed with me again and since that day I felt like I owed Riva something for sticking up for me.

While we waited for the count to be over Riva gone on to tell me about her friends in Brooklyn. When a memorable name flew out her mouth I interrupted.

"Wait a minute did you say Kayla, Kayla Hunter? Dark skin? Nice big ass?"

"Yeah! How da hell you know Kayla?" Riva asked

sort of mystified.

"She's originally from Bridgeport that was my girl back in the days then she moved to BK after her moms got killed."

"Damn it's a small world," Riva smiled in amazement, "ya never know who you're talkin' to in here," Riva said.

"How is Kayla doing anyway?" I asked, as Riva made a funny face.

Riva explained the whole gangsters with a cause thing before she got into how Kayla started robbing people. She sounded kind of jealous, but I knew how she felt cause I was jealous of Kayla too when we used to be together. I just let Riva vent her hatred to make her feel better.

I stuck to Riva like glue for the rest of my bid. I even thought that I was falling in love with her. Early one Saturday morning while everyone else was sleep including the guards, I led Riva into the bathroom. I wanted to show her how much I enjoyed her company.

"What'chu gotta' show me Jaz I'm goin' back to sleep girl," Riva whispered, "It's five-thirty in the morning."

"Let me taste you," I uttered softly, "even your touch excites me," I panted heavy while pulling on her underwear.

Riva was shocked at how forward I was. I made her sit down on the cold toilet seat then forced her legs up. Her feet pressed against the sides of the stall as I went down on her. For this being my first time giving a chick head, it felt natural. Her pink sugar melted in my mouth like cotton candy.

It was dead quiet and the sounds of me lapping labia and clitoris echoed in the bathroom. Riva tasted like a peach soaked in syrup and I consumed each drop as her legs began to shake. Her wetness leaked into my nostrils as booty juice glazed my face. I made her taste herself with a French kiss then afterward we traipsed back to our cube holding hands.

For hours I listened to Riva tell me stories about how she planned to get paid robbing drug dealers like Kayla and them were doing. I thought I was wild, but Riva had me beat with the ideas she came up with.

Up until the last night of my sentence, I hadn't cried once until then.

"So what'chu gonna do when you get outta' here," I asked Riva, "I wish I had someone to go home to I feel so alone."

As the tears began to stream down my cheek, Riva held me close to her chest then caught herself like she was too hard to share emotions.

"I'll punch you in your face if you don't stop crying Jaz. Look here, I'll be in Connecticut for a lil' while, then hopefully I'm goin' back to Brooklyn. You can stay with me for a couple of days until you get right. Now will you stop crying like a lil' bitch? Someone might see us."

"Would you really do that for me?" I perked up, "I'll make it worth your while I promise Riva! All I need to do is find me a job then I'm straight!"

The next morning I got up extra early, anxious to be released. I left everything in my locker. Anyone who wanted those nasty Ramien soups and concord jelly bottles could have them. I waited through one more head count before various names were called to the AP room. Unlike Riva, I still had probation hanging over my head and needed someone to sign me out. Thank god Riva's cousin agreed to do it, or my ass would have still been sitting in there eating hot water gumbo dinners mixed up in garbage bags.

Buck Fifty

As we pulled away from the prison in a beat up Buick Century that I suspected was stolen, since the steering column was necked, I smiled with glee. I didn't give a shit whose car it was, I was just grateful to be on the other side of that fence. Riva was too. She stuck her head out the window to express how happy she was by lifting up her shirt.

"Fuck all you punk ass redneck C.O's," Riva hollered like a cowboy, "yee haw we're outta here bitches!"

Riva's cousin Levitra and I just laughed our asses off as Riva flashed the busload of prisoners that were just pulling in to begin their time. The cold blast of air made me feel light headed for a second, because the ventilation in prison was suffocating. I forgot how nice it was to breathe real air. Off we were.

Levitra lived in Bridgeport all her life and said that it was a complete war zone on her side of town now, full of heartless killers and tedious drug dealers. As soon as we exited the Merritt Parkway Riva had Levitra stop by the nearest gym.

"Yo leave the car runnin'," she uttered before hopping out, "I'll be right back."

At first I couldn't understand why a person would want to hit the gym on their first day out of prison, but about five minutes later I understood the reason very well. Riva came back to the car with like four different credit cards and a pocket full of cash that she stole out of the women's locker room. She said the dummy behind the desk never suspected that she wasn't a club member, because she had on a sweat suit. The prison grays must have given off the impression that Riva worked out there I suppose.

Our next stop was the Trumbull Mall only two minutes away from the gym. This gave us more than enough time to speed shop with the stolen credit cards before they got hot.

"Ai'ight Jaz, you hit Macy's, I'll hit Lord and Taylor and Levitra you hit all the sneaker stores," Riva directed, "get as much as you can, because we don't have that much time before they report their shit missin'. If they ask for I.D play it off like you left it in the car, but don't run out the store whatever you do. Trust me!"

"If you see something cute don't forget my size. I'm a 12," Levitra notified me as she handed over one of the platinum credit cards.

"Let's meet back at the car in a half hour and as soon as you're finished throw the cards in the garbage," Riva insisted.

"Aw'right yo."

The time behind bars destroyed my tan, but being that I looked ghostly pale worked out for me this time. Out of all the stores that I hit not a single employee asked me for I.D. They all assumed that I was just an innocent white girl with good credit even though the name on the card read Kim Jung Chow!

I couldn't believe it when I got back to the car. Between the both of them Riva and Levitra were only able to charge about $500, whereas I alone got away with like $5000 worth of shit. That's when I realized what I had been doing the whole time was wrong. Instead of denying my whiteness, I should have been using it to my advantage. Elvis did it, Eminem did it, and Bill Clinton for example, all surrounded themselves with less fortunate black people to make themselves stand out and look better. At this point I realized that it was time to stop fronting like I was from the hood and start acting more like a white chick. This didn't mean that I still couldn't pull black dudes.

Levitra stopped by a liquor store before driving to her apartment on Hamilton Street. We rushed inside with bags galore then exchanged clothes with each other as we tried on each outfit. While Riva sat on the couch guzzling down the brown juice, I modeled for her in my new satin bra and panties. It felt so good to wear something that actually fit me, unlike those XXL sweat suits and prison uniforms.

"How does this thong look with these low-cut Joey jeans?" I asked Riva with a girly stare.

"Them shits is hot, but they can't fuck wit' these stretch True Religions," Riva shot back.

Riva seemed uninterested in flirting with me for some reason.

"Yo Levitra, call up the bang brothas crew so we can get this party started," Riva hollered into the bathroom, "I was down for eleven months and feel like I could ride eleven dicks!" She laughed

I laughed right along with her, but I was rather insulted that she didn't want me to make her feel good. Here I was thinking this girl was doing favors for me cause she liked me in a sexual way, but Riva hadn't come on to me once since we got out. I wasn't looking for a girlfriend or anything. I just wanted to know what was up so I could move on.

"I thought you said we were going to get drunk and bug out together what's the deal?" I whined upset, "why can't we do our thing baby?"

Riva sucked her teeth then got up off the couch while Levitra talked on the phone with some dude. She called me into the other room to talk in private.

"Look Jaz, I hope you know that what happened between us in there was only for in there? I was bored and you looked lonely, get it? On the brick it's all about the dick, so snap out of it right now. There is no our thing!"

After being told nicely that I was just a prison fling, I got mad and tried to change my demeanor to replicate hers.

"I think I'd rather prefer a dick in my mouth than your tangy twat anyway bitch! You ain't all that," I said as I turned to walk away.

"You a muthafuckin lie!" Riva retorted, "I know if I laid on this bed right now you would drive your tongue right up my ass," Riva laughed with a sneer.

She pulled down her stolen jeans and spread her smooth brown butt cheeks apart to give me a glimpse of her pinkness, knowing I could not resist. When I bent down like a sucker with my eyes half closed and my tongue at full length, Riva turned around and slapped the taste out of my mouth. She hit like a dude and that shit stung.

"I was just testing you! Don't you ever talk to me like that again or I'll slap those plastic lips off your face," she hollered while gripping my throat, "now apologize!"

Riva turned me out in prison and she knew it. I felt so stupid. I stood up with the same reaction as if a guy had dissed me and walked out the room.

"Don't you walk away from me get your white behind back here and apologize to me!"

Like a lost and turned out trick, I walked back in the room and apologized. I felt like I was in no position to be starting shit, so I submitted to Riva's demand.

"I'm sorry" I said, "I don't know what I'm apologizing for, but I'm sorry Riva okay?"

Riva raised her hand to scratch her head, but I flinched thinking she was going to hit me again.

"Relax Jaz, I'm not gonna' hurt you baby I'm

your friend remember?"

Surprisingly, Riva tongue kissed me while gripping my butt with both hands, "and if you're good," Riva whispered in my ear, "just maybe I'll let you eat me out before I leave, but for now keep it on the down low... SSSSHHH."

Riva's split personality made it hard for me to believe her, but when you're confused everything sounds like the truth.

Ten minutes later the doorbell rang. The dudes that Levitra called over showed up. All four of them were tall like professional basketball players and each one of them carried a different brand of liquor in their hands. They took off their jackets then started talking with each other.

"Yo I got that one right there."

"I seen her first though," they argued over who would sleep with Riva.

"Then I'll take shorty with the phatty," another said, referring to me like I was piece of meat being selected at the market.

"Nah we sharin' her!"

After puffing a few blunts and getting bent out of our minds, Levitra and her boyfriend went into the bedroom. Riva let the dude she was with suck on her breasts right in front of me, while the other two guys stood at each end of the couch.

"Two heads are better than one," they laughed dangling their long dicks in my face.

I was drunk about now. Ten months was the longest I had ever went without having a man up in me, so I had some catching up to do. Since Riva didn't want me, I was going to make it worth my while and do both dudes at the same time. I admit that I enjoyed rough anal sex, however my stuff could only stretch but so far before it started hurting.

The next morning my butt hole felt sore as hell. There was mad pain in my drain. It felt like I got fucked with a dildo on the end of a pogo stick. In the shower I had to position myself with my back arched and both cheeks spread apart to let the cool water run over my stuff for relief. Since Riva had got so drunk and passed out in the middle of making out with her jump off, he joined in with his friends on me.

I promised myself that I would never ever let three guys triple team me again, unless I was getting paid big figures.

Hardheads Never Learn

Just because birds of a feather fuck together, doesn't mean they get along. Riva turned out to be a drug-crazed psychopath that only cared about herself. When we weren't bickering over dick, we were fighting over whose turn it was to buy the drugs. The credit card and boosting schemes were not cutting it fast enough for the amounts of coke we sniffed and there was no way I could stay cramped up in Levitra's small apartment too much longer either.

As if we were still inmates with no ambition to do anything else, Riva and I sat on the couch watching Jerry and any other dim-witted talk show while we got high. Levitra was getting sick and tired of Riva and I eating up all of her food without paying. She threatened to put me out if I didn't get a job soon, and since I failed my first urine test my P.O was on my back about finding work too. If I didn't think of something quick I was going to get violated.

Levitra kindly informed me that her job was hiring and suggested that I fill out an application, but I never got around to it.

"If you lazy bitches don't get up off my couch and get a job today I'm sellin' all the gear you boosted last week and I'm kickin' both of y'all the hell outta' here!"

Later on Riva and I sat on the stoop gawking and talking as this uncultivated looking dude named Tony wiped down this hooked up Navigator we never seen before. Riva started a conversation with Tony to see if she could sucker him in for a free ride.

"After you're finished wanna take us for a spin cutie pie?" Riva flirted with the ODB look a like.

"I'll take you for a spin on my dick," the dude joked, as he walked over to where we sat, "I'm only serious," he laughed again, "where you wanna go baby?"

"We don't care. Just anywhere away from here," Riva heaved a sigh, "how bout we ride through P.T. I got some people out there I need to see."

"I'ight bet, I'ma run up in the store right quick and snatch up some blunts... y'all smoke Vega's?"

"Yeah," Riva and I said in unison.

"Okay watch the truck I'll be right back," he said as he walked to the store less than a block away.

While we leaned up against the drug dealer-looking vehicle, this candy girl shows up making a scene.

"You got some nerve showing your face around here?"

"Who she talking to?" Riva wondered out loud.

"I'm talking to that nasty white bitch over there!"

The girl spat, as she gave me a dirty look.

I just laughed in the girl's face, but I was dying to hit her with the keys in my hand. If she weren't holding that baby on the side of her hip I would've slapped her face off just for coming out of her mouth like that.

"Yo I don't even know you" I smirked.

From the way Riva was standing it looked like she was going to hit the girl from behind, so the bitch backed off.

"Oh you wanna jump me now?" The young mother kept pumping up the situation, "I swear! Don't let me catch you by yourself Jaz," Ms resentful threatened as she walked away.

Nobody was going to jump that girl she was bugging. I never seen that chick in my life, but obviously we had a history I forgot about.

"What's she squabbling 'bout?" Tony asked with little concern as he crossed the busy street.

"I don't know jealousy I guess?"

We hopped in the truck with Tony and bounced. The entire time I kept racking my brain trying to remember where I knew that girl from, but nothing came to mind.

"Pull over and park right here" Riva suggested, when we got to the P.T Barnum housing project, "I need something to go with the weed know what I'm saying?"

P.T was one of the worst housing projects in Bridgeport after Father Panic Village got knocked down. P.T was named after the famous and one time mayor of the city, *P.T Barnum*, who was noted for coining the phrase "there's a sucker born every minute."

Riva felt the same way. To her anybody that sold

drugs hand to hand was a sucker and they needed to get got. I knew she had no intention of copping nothing, because I knew she didn't have any money. Riva came out here to beat somebody for a pack. A day before we did the same thing in another project, but Riva never knew when to quit.

"We'll be back in a minute," Riva said to Tony oh so sure, "just promise that you won't leave us."

Tony nodded his head like *why would I leave you?*

Like children with a sweet tooth eager to catch the ice cream man, Riva and I ran from building to building in search of the best crack out. People yelled different brands from every direction we looked.

"Orange... two for tens over here... purple get that purple... Blue bag nickels got dem blue bag nickels... "

"All that shit is garbage," Riva confirmed like she smoked them all before, "I'm looking for my man wit those big ass slabs."

Off to the side of one of the buildings were some children jumping up and down on an old pissy mattress. Contrary to the assumption that these were just little kids playing outside, they all were actually paid lookouts. One of the little niglets whistled a loud birdcall to alert the two drug dealers around the corner that we were coming.

"Yo you sure you know what you're doing?"

"I used to do this all the time around Brooklyn in projects worst than this," Riva whispered, "just do what I told you to do."

"Yo they got weed around the corner," the 16-year-old hustler said while his boy sat back down.

They both assumed that we weren't crack heads because of our youthful good looks.

"That's okay baby I'm looking for what you got. You got dem thangs right?"

"Oh word? Yeah I got dem thangs" the naive pusher asked as he pulled out a whole bundle, "how many you want?"

"That's enough right there in that bag," Riva smiled.

"Oh shit here come the cops!" I yelled to throw them off guard.

Riva put her box cutter to the boy's throat then made him give up his pack before she cut him across the face then ran. His co-worker just stood there in shock. We hauled ass, but got lost between the buildings and had forgot where Tony parked.

"No Riva this way," I yelled after spotting Tony's truck by the playground.

Just as I said that I had seen this dude point and yell, "THERE THEY GO RIGHT THERE!"

Riva looked at me and I looked at her and we started running faster. Five dudes with assault weapons in their hands chased us back to Tony's truck.

"Hurry up! Pull off!" I shrieked over and over, "they're coming pull off!"

"BLLA'DAAT! BLLA'DAAT! BLLA'DAAT!"

"Ahhh!"

Tony got hit then slumped over the steering wheel. I could hear the sound of bullets bouncing off the truck, as I stayed crouched down between the front and back seats. Small pieces of window glass were all over my head and shit. I thought there is no way we're going to make out of this one alive. The entire ordeal seemed to last an eternity, but in actually it all went down in less than a minute.

In a flash Riva kicked Tony's body out the door

and sped away in his Truck. She floored the gas striking one of the shooters as he stood in front of us firing his weapon. It was hard for Riva to control the steering doing 85 mph, because one of the tires got shot out. Tony had a large P-90 under his seat that slid into view when Riva slammed on the breaks. I grabbed the bundle of crack first then tossed the commando looking gun up front.

We thought we had lost them, until gunfire echoed beneath the I-95 underpass. The traffic jam on State Street was ugly. We were blocked in. Riva jumped out of one side of the truck and I jumped out of the other. She ran her way and I ran mine, as the shots never let up.

"BUCK! BUCK! BUCK! BUCK! BUCK!"

Out of nowhere unmarked Crown Victoria's rolled up. Police wearing thin nylon jackets with the letters TNT displayed on the back, blocked the exit and entrance ramp to I-95. They had all the escape routes covered. Since there were so many other people running for cover I slipped right through the commotion. People scattered like roaches as the shooting continued. Riva wasn't so inconspicuous since she had a big gun in her hand fleeing the scene. I'll give it up to Riva though she went out gangsta!

"BLLOOOM! BLLOOOM! BLLOOOM! BLLOOOM! BLLOOOM! BLLOOOM! BLLOOOM! BLLOOOM! BLLOOOM"

Riva lit it up like the fourth of July. Bullets hit everything and everybody as she waved Tony's Sub-machine gun in a 180-degree blast radius. She hit some of the dealers that were shooting at us, but also hit bystanders too. Riva laid one dude out spread eagle on the hood of somebody's car with smoke streaming from his chest. Another one of the missile like rounds ripped right through a cops vest like cotton.

Police were shooting at the drug dealers as well as shooting at Riva. I covered my mouth in shock when I seen Riva get hit. It looked like she was doing the Harlem shake from the way the bullets tore through her womanly frame. In the last breath of her life Riva stuck up her middle finger at the cops then finally collapsed.

Ignorant to my role in the event the Police ushered me off to the side with the rest of the innocent bystanders. Chaotic would be the best word to describe the crowds of shaken up onlookers. All of the dealers who could identify my face were dead. But I wasn't out of the clear just yet. As I walked away picking glass out of my hair, I prayed that no one pointed me out or involved me in their stories to the cops. I made it all the way to Park Avenue on foot, before catching the bus back to Hamilton Street.

"What am I going to say to Levitra?" I thought while I waited for her to come home from work, *"I can't believe Riva is gone."*

I felt like just packing my bags and leaving but unless I wanted to get violated, I couldn't leave Connecticut.

Days passed and I was still sleeping on Levitra's couch believe it or not. With Riva dead I knew my welcome was more than worn out. Levitra gave me exactly one week to get my shit straight or I was out on the street. I had to almost literally kiss her ass until I could find a place of my own.

When the time came I sat inside the funeral home with Levitra and the rest of Riva's family members that showed up for the service. Out of all her friends from Brooklyn, this chick named Jackie was the only one who showed up. We talked for a while and exchanged numbers before Jackie hopped in some fancy car with some dude and they left. She told me to look her up when I was ever in the city.

Ironically the reverend that gave Riva's eulogy was the same reverend we would bump into copping coke. I don't think anyone else knew that he sniffed on the low, because they seemed to be listening to the bullshit he was putting down about the ramifications of drug abuse. He had some nerve I'll tell you.

The sermon was long. Levitra went outside to get some air and I followed behind her after tossing a rose in Riva's coffin. One of Levitra's cousins from out of town had a big bottle of Hennessy that he wanted to drink in Riva's honor, so we sat in his Caddy drinking the pain away. Levitra's cousin was the type to get all philosophical on you and shit when he drank.

"You know what cuz we some dumb ass ma'fuckas," Levitra's cousin uttered after he took a swig of Henny.

"What'chu talking 'bout Monk I consider myself an intelligent black woman you must mean *you're* a dumb muthafucka not me," Levitra retorted.

"What I'm saying is why do we kill and rob each other for a piece of paper that ain't worth a damn? What we call the almighty dollar is in fact a Federal Reserve note. It doesn't even have any real value cause it ain't even backed by gold or silver anymore. It's a promissory note promising to pay, like a fiend promises to pay after some sucka' ass serves him," Monk doubled up another gulp,

"...And the Federal Reserve ain't even *Federal* it's a privately owned banking system controlled by old white niggas that run the entire world's economy and power structure. They create debt through inflation and every time we spend a dollar we're legally promising to pay that amount... you should know Levitra you work at a bank right? It's like writing a check against a closed account. What happens is her, me, you and the rest of us dumb muthafuckas in this country end up owing the Federal Reserve Bank...it's called the national debt. That's why they call money currency, cause just like electrical current it makes shit operate and do whatever the hell they want us to do."

"What does that have to do with our cousin lying in a casket up in there?" Levitra gasped, "your right I do work at the bank and I never heard anything about that, so pass the Henny and shut the hell up! We tryna' get fucked up, not take over the government."

Monk realized neither one of us was interested in hearing what he had to say, so he emptied the rest of the Henny on the ground for Riva then kicked us out the Caddy. At the time I didn't understand what Monk was saying, but now I do. Money is the illusion of power. It's what you do with it that makes you powerful or not. Church.

Insufficient Funds

Surprisingly I actually got the job at the bank where Levitra worked. The manager thought I resembled his wife in the early years of their marriage and practically hired me before even filling out an application. Most times I would diss older white guys, because they reminded me of my father, but I charmed this one to get special treatment. To separate myself from the other birds that worked there, I dropped all the slang and spoke like an educated suburbanite.

Working for the first time in my life wasn't all that bad like I expected. All I did was count money and snoop into people's business all day. I honestly enjoyed working at the bank. Everything was going fine, until two weeks into the job this black Expedition with dark tints pulls into my drive-thru window. At first I didn't think anything of it until the driver laid on the horn like an idiot.

"One moment please," I scowled as I completed the last transaction, "Good morning how can I help you today?"

The window came down slowly and a shiny pistol appeared. I almost shit my draws when I heard Burner's voice through the intercom,

"You owe me Jaz and I swear if you don't give it to me that's it! Come by the old block. You know where I be at," he said, and then his face and gun disappeared in the tint.

Burner sounded serious. He didn't even give me a chance to make up an excuse as to how and why Chiffon took his money. I forgot to mention that when I was messing with Duane I spent Burner's hard earned money on some raw shit that made my jaw move side to side like Sammy Davis, Jr. I planned on paying Burner back, I did, but I didn't plan on getting shot or going to jail though.

Here I was making $9.00 an hour at the bank and now I had to pay this nigga too, fuck that. Something had to give. The thought of ignoring Burner crossed my mind a few times, but he was too deep in the streets to hide from. Plus now he knew where I worked. I wondered if he knew where I lived too?

"Where in the hell am I gonna get $2000 from?" I asked myself over and over again, "I'm just starting to get on my feet shit!"

In the past I always robbed Peter to pay Paul, so somebody was going to get it, know what I mean?

As the next customer pulled up to the drive-thru window I sat there in deep thought worrying about how not to get shot again.

"Good morning Mrs. Goldstein would you like your balance?" I snapped out of my thinking dilemma.

"Yes I would dear thank you," the old Jewish woman replied caressing her mink coat while she waited.

Mrs. Goldstein always deposited at least $4000 into her account every Wednesday since I worked at the bank. When I read that she had a balance of $94,136.07 on my computer screen I almost choked.

"One minute Mrs. Goldstein?" I stalled for time, "our computers are slow today."

After reading all of her private information I said, "have a nice day," as I sent the balance statement through the air tube.

The entire time I was plotting on how I was going to jack Mrs. Goldstein's old Zionist ass. Being that the cameras were on me, I memorized her home address until I was able to write it down in the restroom. Working at the bank gave me access to all types of personal information and I could also cash stolen checks at will if I wanted to. All I had to do now was figure out how and when to make my move.

On my lunch break I snorted the last little bit of blow I had with me. 4:00pm came around and it was time to finally punch out. Usually I rode home with Levitra, but she was off today, so I took the city bus to the address I had written down in the restroom. I got off the bus holding the piece of paper in my hand, looking like a tourist as I walked up and down Park Avenue north until I found the right address.

Soon I spotted Mrs. Goldstein's Lexus parked in the driveway. The front door was cracked and all the lights in the house were on. I had to see if the old lady lived alone, before I did anything else. When I peeked through the side window I heard Mrs. Goldstein talking to her cats then I left.

The next night I had Levitra drop me off a block

away from Mrs. Goldstein's house. Of course I didn't tell Levitra what I was up to, because I didn't want that nosey chatterbox up in my business.

"I'll see you later thanks for the ride," I hopped out in a hurry.

"Thanks for the ride my ass," Levitra held out her hand, "I need money for gas gurl where you think you goin'?"

I gave Levitra my last $20 then slammed her piece of shit car door hoping that it fell off in the middle of the street.

Looking suspicious was of no concern to me. In this neighborhood the only camouflage needed was white skin. College girls that looked like me were always seen jogging around the area, so that's how I dressed. I froze my ass off in spandex runner tights and I must have jogged around the block ten times before I moved in for the attack. Given that I only scoped out the place once, I prayed that no one else was in the house, because I didn't have a gun.

Quickly I crept to the back of the one floor ranch style home to make sure it was clear. Mrs. Goldstein was on the phone, so I waited underneath the patio deck until she got off. Every little noise startled me. An ambulance siren in the area set off all the more paranoia. Finally I walked up the steps on edge before ringing the bell. I remember the butterfly's turning in my stomach.

"Hello... who is it?" Mrs. Goldstein merrily voiced from inside.

I took off running. While she went to the front door to see who it was, I ran to the back door again and snuck inside. Mrs. Goldstein was startled half to death when she reentered the kitchen. Her facial expression changed in an instant. She looked at me oddly backing away as I moved forward without saying anything.

"You're that girl from the bank!" She flinched, "What in the hell are you doing in my home! Get out right now or I am calling the police!"

I took the kitchen phone off the hook while approaching with my hands out to choke the bitch.

"You ain't calling nobody," I growled.

"Oh my god!" Mrs. Goldstein stifled, "I-can't-breathe!"

"Where's the purse?" I demanded to know as I released my grip, "I know you got money bitch. WHERE'S THE MONEY!"

"Help!" She cried out as soon as I let go, "HELP ME SOMEONE PLEASE!"

For a senior citizen Mrs. Goldstein put up one hell of a struggle. The phone was making that irritating off the hook sound, while she tried to run out the backdoor. I snatched her from behind to shut the old bag up and then grabbed a rolling pin off the kitchen table. I beat on Mrs. Goldstein's head like a wild drummer until she collapsed on the floor.

The flour on the wooden roller absorbed some of the blood, but my hands were dripping with it. Bloody fingerprints seemed to appear everywhere and I began to panic. At first I tried to clean up the mess than said fuck it. I didn't even search the house like I planned. I just grabbed what was in sight. The purse was sitting on the kitchen counter, so I rummage through it with the quickness and lucked up.

Some people write down their PIN numbers so they don't forget and Mrs. Goldstein happened to be one of them. Her four-digit access code was written on the back of the slipcover that enclosed the card. I didn't have time to go through every little compartment, so I took the whole damn purse, even though I only needed the checkbook and her drivers' license.

Before stuffing the motionless body in the closet, I removed Mrs. Goldstein's wedding and engagement rings from her fingers. Hanging up was a full-length mink coat that felt even more comfy than the Chinchilla Duane gave me. It must have been my lucky day, because I also found two winning $50 scratch offs in the pocket.

It was time to split. I backed out the driveway in the old lady's Lex hoping no one heard the screams.

"That wasn't so hard," I thought to myself, while standing at a 24 hour ATM counting cash.

Like with most debit cards, for the sake of the customer's security, Mrs. Goldstein's card had a daily withdrawal limit of only $400. My plan was to write out big checks anyway, but I needed some cash to pay Burner before he put a slug in my head. A few days later I pulled up on the Ave like I was doing the damn thing. As I pulled up in the shiny Lexus, all the niggas on the block nodded to the sounds of Raekwon's Purple Tape... "*Peace Connecticut*!"

"Yo anybody seen Burner?" I asked around as one of his snot nose dealers sold me a bag of weed and a twenty of blow. Burner moved up since the last time I saw him. He was a boss of his own block now.

"He 'cross the street," the kid answered, examining my twenties as if they were fake.

I wasn't really worried about the car, so I left the shit running with the system pumping when I walked over to where Burner was playing cards. I don't know if it was the fur coat, or if I was just nervous, but my forehead was sweating like a pig and it was freezing outside.

"You betta' have my money or that mink is my

girlfriend's new grocery store coat," Burner said as his eyes stayed focused on the deck, "matter of fact I should just take that shi for the hell of it!"

Burner looked upset. Some dude was ripping him in Black Jack. In the short amount of time I stood there, Burner must have lost almost a thousand dollars. I was ready to go, so I handed Burner his money before lighting my third cigarette in the last five minutes. Burner didn't even count the cash I passed him. He just started laying bets right away only to lose it all in one hand.

"As you can see Jaz it ain't about the money it's about the fact you tried to play me," Burner barked at me, "there's still something else you owe me," he said as he grabbed his crotch.

I knew exactly what he was referring to now. He was still upset about that day we went to the city and I didn't give him any booty after he ate me out. Customarily if I ever stepped on the block 12 O' clock at night, I was usually looking for one of two things, drugs, dick or sometimes both. This time however, I just wanted to be by myself.

Burner forced me to drive to some place in Stratford, Connecticut, not too far from the block. It was only ten minutes out of the city, but even so I didn't want to go. I felt that if I didn't Burner would do something bad to me. Burner had no clue that he was riding in a stolen car and if we got pulled over I was saying he stole it and made me drive.

"Lighten up Jaz," Burner smiled, "I ain't gonna hurt you baby I was just playing when I seen you at the bank."

"No you weren't you were dead serious I know you," I said as I parked the car, "where are you taking me Burner?"

"Chill it's a surprise," he said.

"If you go in that house with him you might not ever come out," said the voice in my head. I was extremely on edge.

"Well I don't like surprises," I twisted my face, "I ain't going in there Burner. No fuck that I'm not going in there. Do you think I'm just going to' let you kill me."

I felt like that lady in the movie *Goodfellas* when Robert De Niro asked her to walk into that abandoned store front, so he could have her whacked.

Seconds later after Burner closed his cell, this white girl around my age came to the door and waved us inside.

"Who's that Marsha Brady looking bitch?"

"That's Susan she's just this freak that goes both ways, I thought we could have some fun together, you still owe me ya know?"

"Was that your surprise? You had me drive all the way over here for a ménage, Burner, you're crazy you know that," I laughed a load of stress away.

Though I still didn't trust Burner, I felt a little bit more comfortable and willingly went inside.

"Nice fur," Susan complemented as she hung up my coat on the hook for me, "hmmm... classy I likes, she flashed a thumbs up before introducing herself, "and hi there I'm Susan nice to meet you."

"Can I use your bathroom?" I asked, as I gave Susan the cold shoulder.

"Down the hall to your left," she pointed.

I sat on the toilet wondering how did I get myself in this situation. I figured Burner wouldn't leave me alone until I gave him some long awaited pussy, so I decided to play along and enjoy what they had in store for me.

"Jaz come in the bedroom I want you to see this," Burner called out to me.

Wow and I thought I was a freak? Susan was bizarre. When I walked in the bedroom Susan was sniffing a line of coke off of Burner's hard on. I had to laugh when she made her pussy smoke a cigarette. The bitch was out there!

"Come on baby take off your clothes... let us see them big fun bags you got under there" Susan nervously squirmed from the enjoyable thought of sucking my breast.

Burner was enjoying it all as he rolled up a coke laced blunt. While me and Susan rubbed titties together, he used the empty Garcia Vega tube as a dildo on her.

"This is for my homies," I giggled, before spilling the cognac on Burner's cock.

"I bet you can't swallow the whole thing?" He delightfully challenged, as Susan's head moved back and forth on his dick like a chicken. Susan was so good at smoking pole Burner ejaculated in less than a minute.

"You two stay right here and have fun with each other while I go take a piss," Burner declared.

Ten minutes later, while my ass was arched up in the air, licking cocaine from Susan's belly, I let out an ear splitting scream.

"AAAAAAAAAAAAAAHHHHHHHHHHHHH," I Cried like a baby.

The smell of burnt pubic hair filled the room instantly. To my surprise, there stood the girl who was talking shit to me a few weeks ago. Instead of holding a baby this time she was holding a hot curling iron. Then in walked Chiffon Davis and I almost shit the bed.

"Surprise Beotch! Remember me! I know you had something to do with Duane's murder and tonight you're going to join him in hell!"

Now I recalled where I knew that girl. Kim was her name. She was the one with Chiffon the day Duane and I got caught doing it on his car.

"It seems like I always catch you with your pants down," Chiffon commented as she pulled out a pair of sharp barber scissors.

I shivered with fear as I held my crotch in excruciating pain. Chiffon and Kim stomped and kicked me first. I could not believe that this was happening all over again. My eyes quickly filled with tears as Chiffon began to cut off my hair.

"Don't just cut off her hair, stab that bitch in her head!" Kim encouraged, but Chiffon didn't get the chance to do so.

Susan had smashed a lamp over Chiffon's head as she fled out the bedroom. I jumped up with all the strength I had and fought with Kim out the door. She came at me with a rotisserie fork, but I blocked it with one of Susan's dirty dishes in the sink. I caught Kim with a lucky right hook knocking her to the floor then I grabbed Mrs. Goldstein's fur that was hanging up by the door.

There I was butt naked three in the morning running down the freezing pavement with a fur in my hand screaming like Paul Revere. If Burner would have been thorough in setting me up, he would have took the fur coat or the car keys when he deserted us. I would've really been done for then.

If I were a cat my nine lives would have been up at this point. I drove without direction and ended up at Seaside Park where I cried myself to sleep. I awoke to a bright light shining in my face. It was a police officer tapping his flashlight on the glass. Something told me to pull off, but instead I hesitated.

"The Park is closed ma'am what are you doing here at this time of morning?" The officer asked.

He pointed his light throughout the car as I let down the window, "May I see some I.D?" He probed.

"I'm sorry officer I don't have any on me right now, I think I left my purse at home."

"What's your name?" The young Spanish cop pressed on, "how about registration and insurance do you at least have that?

"Sure. My name is um, Sandra, Sandra Goldstein. This is my grandmother's car," I started crying again, "I know it was wrong officer, but she doesn't know that I have her car. I snuck out of the house this morning to be with my boyfriend."

At this point I started sobbing like a scared little a girl. I thought I was going down for sure.

"See, officer my grandmother forbids me to see my boyfriend because I'm Jewish and he's Puerto Rican like you are. See I love Carlos and all I wanted to do was see him before he leaves for the Army tomorrow."

I got out of the car and threw myself at the cop. I fell into his grasp as I wept on his shoulders. I presumed that he was Puerto Rican, because he looked like Mark Anthony without glasses. If he didn't have sympathy for me and my bullshit story it was game over.

"That's terrible," he shook his head appalled, "when I was young I experienced the same racist bullshit with my first girlfriend. I loved her but her father hated me because I was from a poor Latino section of town... look you look like a nice girl Sandy, so I'm not going to run you in. Just be careful and take the car straight home okay."

The officer walked me back to the car and closed the door for me. I couldn't believe he went for it. My pouting lips and sad blue eyes did him in. The dumb spic even gave me a tissue before pacing back to his cruiser sulking in his own thoughts.

"Whew! That was close," I released a deep breath of relief as I drove to Levitra's barefoot.

I was tired as hell and had to be to work in less than four hours. I convinced Levitra that it would be most beneficial to her if she submitted the falsified checks at my drive-up window that day and that day only.

"If this works Levitra, you'll have gees in your pocket and I'll be out of your crib tonight!"

In exchange for Mrs. Goldstein's wedding rings and half of whatever amount of money we scammed, Levitra agreed to play the role.

9:15 A.M Levitra pulled up in my lane like a normal customer.

"Can I help you?" I acted real cool, looking a hot mess with my unwanted new hairstyle.

"Yes I'd like to cash a check please," Levitra spoke into the intercom.

"No problem ma'am large bills or small?" I said with a straight face.

The Puerto Rican girl working next to me recognized Levitra's hoop ride, but she didn't say anything.

"The Bigger the betta'!" Levitra's hood voice over came her weak impersonation.

I ran the check through the system like I would any other, "okay" I said, "you're all set Mrs. Goldstein have a nice a day!"

Five minutes later we worked the same routine.

Levitra made the first check out to cash for $6000 and the second one the same. It was that easy. We could have run this scam until Mrs. Goldstein's account was drained, but after the second trip, Levitra hadn't returned in hours.

I was beginning to think that she ran off with the money, until strangely enough my computer screen shut down. Everyone else's computer worked fine except mine. I looked around the bank and noticed the manager's door was cracked open. The Puerto Rican girl that worked next to me was in the office. The manager was staring at me intently as he spoke on the phone with someone before closing the door with his foot. The lethargic security guard that stood at the front door came rushing over to my station soon after.

"Mr. Roberts would like to speak with you in his office right away."

"Why is something wrong?" I acted concerned.

"I don't know. He told me to escort you to his office lets go."

With a pocketbook strap over my shoulder and keys in my hand, I left my post and followed the rent-a-cop like I was actually going to go with him. Coming into the bank through an entrance on the other side was Burner with you know who? I guess she was ready to finish what she started last night I presume.

I bailed out the other exit as customers entered the bank. Realizing I had escaped out the side door, Mr. Roberts and the fat security guard chased me to the car. I hauled ass out of that parking lot, like I just robbed the place, flooring it all the way to the highway as police passed me going the opposite direction.

What I didn't know at the time, was that Levitra had got caught trying to write out a check at some top-notch jewelry store. When the police tried to notify Mrs. Goldstein about the stolen checkbook they had recovered, Levitra got scared and snitched on me about everything that she knew. One thing led to another and they soon discovered Mrs. Goldstein's body.

On The Run

Instead of ditching the stolen Lexus right away, I drove to my grandmother's house in Mt. Vernon, NY. After wiping off my prints I abandoned the car in a rough part of Yonkers. At this point in my life I should have learned my lesson and head out to California, even if I had to hitch hike, but I stayed on the east coast anyway like a damn fool.

Until things calmed down, I figured I'd chill at granny O'Reilly's spot for a minute. Granny wasn't rich or nosey like my other grandmother in Cali, but she was cool because she didn't bother me with questions. I hadn't seen her since my father's funeral, but I remember my sister telling me that granny suffered with a slight case of Alzheimer's disease or something. To me that just meant I could tell her forgetful mind anything.

Living with a senior citizen wasn't too bad. Basically I came and went as I seen fit. All granny seemed to do was sit in her room and watch Law & Order, so she rarely got in the way. However on some days granny would forget who I was. If I didn't remind her that I was her son's youngest daughter Jasmine, she would have called the police about a stranger roaming the house. I had to play it cool when she became absentminded. The only rules granny enforced sane or senile was that I clean up after myself and pay for the groceries I use.

To avoid the police I only went out at night. Conveniently Sue's Rendezvous, a strip club where Riva's friend Jackie supposedly worked at, was only a few minutes away from where granny lived. So every other evening I would stop in Sue's hoping I would catch Jackie, but I never did. However I found something else that interested me.

"Hi I'll take a double shot of Hennessy and a Heineken," was the first thing out of my mouth each time I hit the bar.

"I'm sorry honey, I know your new, but we're not allowed to serve the dancers while they're working," the bubble butt bartender replied, "it's policy."

"Oh sweetie, I don't work here," I said while checking out her luscious booty, which was way bigger than mine, "I'm just looking for a friend. Do you know if Jackie is dancing tonight?"

"Jackie? Never heard of her, but if you're looking for a *friend* my name's Vanessa," the bartender winked and licked her lips before serving me my drinks.

I could see why Vanessa thought I was a new dancer, because my melons were bulging through the low cut top I wore and the rest of my outfit looked stripperish as well. You should have seen all the guys swoon over the bar when I arched my back to stretch.

Meanwhile a fat white man dressed in an old dingy pasta stained tee shirt sat down on the stool next to mine. He slid me a $50 bill as I downed a shot of cognac.

"I heard you say you're looking for a friend" fatso smiled silly, "how much for a lap dance?"

It was flattering that everyone thought I looked sexy like the girls on stage, but talking to this dude was not a good look. He was the epitome of a slime ball pervert.

"Since you were snooping in my conversation so hard, you must have heard me say I DON'T WORK HERE ASSHOLE!" I snapped at the depraved son of a bitch before throwing his money at the stage.

As I got up to move I purposely spilled the jerks drink. Shortly after, this clean cut Italian who later identified himself as the man in charge approached me. He stared down at my thigh as I adjusted my mini skirt to sit down.

"What's this? I notice you always come in then leave all the time. What's up? Can I interest you in a job? We could always use a pretty girl like yourself."

"Um not really," I responded more friendly than I did with the last guy, "does the job you're referring to have blow at the beginning?" I smiled with conjecture.

"Hey I don't know what Vanessa told you, but whateva' she said it's all true," he amused the other bartenders, "but seriously doll I run a respectable business here," he seemed to convince himself.

"I think I'll stay on this side of the bar for now" I rebuffed the offer.

"Okay, but it's your loss babe. And don't forget this is a strip bar, so take it easy on my customers doll."

"Wait a minute!" I grabbed his arm right before he walked away, "How much money are we talking?"

"A helluva'lot!" He looked me up and down again, "who wouldn't pay to see those cans? My name's Vinny step into my office so I can tell you how it works in private."

As we walked into Vinny's office we passed the real owner in the hallway. He overheard me doubting myself about being on stage and gave a few words of encouragement.

"You're gonna' knock 'em dead in here beautiful are you kidding me!" The old man laughed as he escorted another newcomer to the exit.

When the old man walked back into Vinny's office I stuck out my hand to greet him. He ignored me and told Vinny to take a hike before closing the door.

"Hi again, I'm Jaz," I said with a mega-watt smile.

"Hi... Kneel."

"Nice to meet you Neil, I just love your club by the way it's so_"

"My name isn't Neil darling, it's Tony I mean kneel, as in get down on your knees and show me what you got."

The boss tested out my skills, by how well I sucked his shriveled up salami. It was nauseating, but at least I made $400 for the two minutes I pleasured the geezer.

The next thing I know I'm on stage the following week squeezing half a dozen ping-pong balls out of my ass. All in all I stayed on the lam from the Bridgeport police department, stripping the winter away through spring. I still hadn't run into anyone I knew though. Not until the popular "Shake Off" contest, where girls from one state compete with one another on who's got the best wiggles and jiggles.

In Sue's my name was *Emmanuelle* and up on stage I was an erotic beast. Men went crazy as other girls tried to compete with me by picking up beer bottles with their vaginas, but I was a natural at my routine. Every Tuesday the spot stayed rammed with music moguls down to local corner thugs, and they all spent major paper, but for the shake off it was trump tight.

For a negotiable fee the biggest tippers got to pull a string of beads out my ass. Each time my eyes would roll back in ecstasy as men and women watched with elation. In no time, a cascade of cash would rain down on my booty. Cha' Ching! On my first big night I made over $3000 in tips alone, which the other dancers told me wasn't shit compared to what I could make after the club tricking. Honestly I was content dancing and wasn't interested in selling my body just yet. I had already made enough money over the winter to finance a used SL 55 AMG Mercedes Benz, which I registered in my grandmother's name.

"Get your dolla's ready!" The DJ announced as I walked out of the dressing room to the music of Rick James Super freak one Tuesday night in May.

"Coming to the stage we have a bunny rabbit with a naughty habit... the eighth wondah of the worlddddd! Emmanuelle! The human ping pong machine!"

While the crowd clapped their hands in excitement, in walks Jackie with a dude on her arm as they took a seat at the bar. I watched her come in from the mirror, but she didn't notice me until I turned around.

"Oh shit!" Jackie covered her mouth surprised

yet excited, "I know that girl," I read her lips, as she stared at me with prompt stimulation.

I worked my signature move for her and her friend in the same way I would for any other couple tipping fifty's. Like always, heads crowded around to see me do my thing. They showered me with bills as the oiled ping-pong balls slowly popped out of my ass one by one. Jackie's boyfriend must have been amazed, because his mouth hung wide open. After I finished my set, I came back out to meet and greet the rappers in V.I.P before going over to holler at Jackie.

All I could do was smile, "aren't you gonna introduce me to your sexy boyfriend?"

"Not until you tell us how you fit all those balls up your ass!" We all laughed.

Jackie thought I looked cute with my hair cut short, but she had the best low cut fade in the entire bar. I liked her vibe. She was more animated than Riva, but seemed to be more even-tempered. More down to earth you know? I felt like I knew her for years from all the stories Riva told, but you really don't know someone until you know them.

We laughed over the loud music and ordered more drinks while we entertained each other's conversation.

"I would have never thought about stripping if I didn't come in here all the time looking for you. I thought you said you worked here?"

"I do kinda' work here, but I never told you I danced here," Jackie grinned, while she made a gun shape with her hand, "lets just say I get money in here."

"Hey, what'chu doin' after this?" Jackie's boyfriend asked, like he was interested in me, "We got a room in Manhattan what's up? Lets have some fun cause money's no object to us. We got doe for days so don't worry I'll take care of you."

"Actually *they* got a room," Jackie pointed over her shoulder to a bunch of hustlers popping bottles, "you wanna roll wit me?"

"I don't know yo, I don't know," I paused with second thoughts of Riva getting shot, "my body is kinda' sore, I been dancing all night, plus I heard how you get down and I'm not trying to get killed over no petty niggas" I whispered in Jackie's ear.

"Dem niggas got doe and we about to get paid! You ain't gotta' fuck nobody," Jackie whispered, "You think I like this kid? I just met this dude outside."

Even though I promised God I would never ever rob and kill again after escaping the Bridgeport PD, I left the club with Jackie around 3:30 A.M anyway. We followed a black Suburban with Pennsylvania plates to the Bronx River Parkway in my freshly painted pink Mercedes Benz. At 4:15 A.M we pulled up to the Hilton in Manhattan. Jackie got out while I parked a block away.

In the elevator the alleged ballers were all over us like they never hit ass. Even the hardest looking one got giddy and anxious in anticipation of getting laid.

"Slow your roll big boy! Ain't nothin' poppin' off until we see some paper," Jackie announced.

"Money ain't a thing shorty, how much you need to get it crunk?" The driver asked, as he flung one-dollar bills up in the air again.

It was apparent that we had these dudes wide open. Out of town niggas were always the sweetest to get, because they were too trusting and too playful. They never saw it coming. The moment we entered room 112, I took my shirt off to distract them. Jackie excused herself and went to the bathroom to supposedly freshen up. While all three guys fondled my breasts with joy, thinking they had found some freaks to bang, Jackie burst back in the room waving a gun.

"You know what it is! Everybody on the muthafuckin' floor" she yelled, "or yo ass is gon die!"

"Hold on wait, let's talk about this shorty," one of the suckers pleaded, "I got a wife and kids!"

"Shut up! Get your ass on the floor!"

As I searched their pockets I frowned in disappointment.

"I know this ain't all you got? Where's the rest of it?" Jackie shoved the dude crying, before slapping him in the head with the knot of ones I found in his pocket.

"The rest is over there wrapped up in the towel by the lamp, just don't shoot us!"

"Yo this ain't shit!" I scowled in complete frustration as I undid the towel with about $3000 in it.

"You should've never fronted like you had big chips" Jackie smirked as she placed a pillow to one of their heads, "I wish it didn't have to be like this cutie... POP!"

I tried to stop her, but Jackie shot the other two the same way just as fast. We got the hell out of there we thought without being seen. If them dudes didn't front like they were big time drug dealers, they probably would have still been alive. For a measly $3000 to split two ways, the whole thing was a waste of time. More than that I put my freedom on the line for Jackie and she made her judgment look bad. Hell I made more money in a thirty minutes twirling on a pole.

About two days after the botched robbery Jackie and this dude named Omar, were getting skeed up with me in my grandmother's living room. When I went into the kitchen to wash the residue off the mirror Omar summoned me back into the living room like something was extremely wrong.

"Police need your help in finding a pair suspects in a triple homicide. The two women seen here were caught on camera with these three men who were later found shot to death execution style in their Manhattan hotel suite two days ago. Security cameras at the Hilton show the victims exiting an elevator with two women who were dressed as prostitutes. Sources report that the women were seen fleeing the scene only minutes after hotel employees heard gunfire. The victims Ron Gibbs, Oshea Johnson and Jack Orlando all suffered gunshot wounds to the back of the head. Gibbs was an up and coming rapper out of Philadelphia, while Johnson and Orlando were both listed as Brooklyn residents with criminal records. If you have any information police ask that you call the TIP hotline shown on the screen below... and in other news..."

Seeing my face on the news was scary. Despite the video resolution being a little fuzzy, my face was more recognizable than Jackie's because she wore large shades. Maybe that's why Jackie didn't seem to care as much as I did. Come on I mean damn, a fucking surveillance tape with your face on it is played on the news and the first thing you think about is how good your outfit looked? Get the fuck out of here!

Maybe if I wasn't already wanted in Connecticut for lets see, violating probation, bank robbery, Arson and a couple of murders, I might have felt more relaxed.

"What the hell did they mean prostitutes?"

Jackie went on with the bullshit, "maybe you did, but I ain't look like no fuckin' prostitute!"

"Bitch I don't give a fuck how you looked! Don't you understand what this means!" I yelled at Jackie, "I'm hit! They couldn't really see your face so you don't give a shit, but I do. I'm hotter than a beach cooked pussy now cause of you. I got a fucking life and I'm not going back to fucking jail."

"Listen to you," Jackie chuckled, "*I'm not go-ing back to fuck-ing-jail I got a fuck-ing-life.* You said that like a true white girl what happened to your accent phony?"

"Kiss my ass you're the phony you ain't no gangster. You're just a dumb cokehead with a gun. I swear if I get caught over this, man I can't even drive my car now," I complained until totally losing it.

Jackie and I tussled before Omar broke it up. I got in the last slap, so Jackie kept talking junk.

"Fuck that Mary Kay looking shit anyway" Jackie hated on me, "if you get caught it's because you let yourself get caught! I ain't make you come with me dat night."

"If I were you Jaz I would get some hair dye and a fake I.D. Keep my nose clean and stay out the limelight and handle my business. I got this Mexican that can get you any kind of papers you need. For the right price I could even get you an entirely new identity."

Omar had me thinking. A new identity was probably the only way I could escape all the trouble I was in and start living my life like a bona fide white chick again.

"What exactly is the 'right price?"

"I dunno," Omar scratched his head uncertain, "about fifteen geez maybe less?"

"How fast can they get me what I need?" I delved in more, totally blocking Jackie out of the conversation.

"It depends on how fast you can get the money I guess. I got the number at home I'll call Charlie tomorrow and set up a meting. In the meantime what are you gonna' do about work?"

Omar seemed like he could be valuable to me after all, but his overly concerned attitude bothered me. As for Jackie she turned out to be more trouble than she was worth. She was a fucking pest I swear. I couldn't go anywhere or do anything without hoe happy Jackie tagging along and leeching off of me.

Omar called his ID connection the next day and he convinced me to quit dancing at Sue's. Omar said a place like Sue's drew too much attention. Instead he said he knew another strip bar that was much more under the radar. Omar was like Duane. He thought he could pimp me, so I let him think I was easy to fool just to see how far he would go.

You would never know by just taking the train or driving to work or simply observing the scene, but there are vampires patrolling the streets of New York day and night in search of their next prey. They can tell if you're underage or if you're merely out past your curfew looking for some fun. These types of guys are trained to notice the girls who could barely walk in heels or the ones who apply extra makeup just to look older.

In the blink of an eye runaways and rebellious girls are taken off the streets then put to work never to be seen by their families again. Sometimes they show up on the Internet with a dick in their mouths, but more times than most they end up in dumpsters. Omar was one of these modern day vampires. He worked for various strip club owners looking for new girls to turn out or better yet slave. The best girls to catch were the runaways who happened to be in trouble with the law, because a girl in trouble with the law is cut off from society. The chances of a girl like that going to the police for help were slim to none.

For me Omar was easy to spot, regardless of the sardonic gold tooth fangs he wore. When Omar came in Sue's he stood out to me, because any man who comes in a strip club that doesn't drink or get a lap dance and doesn't even get excited when he sees a beautiful naked girl gyrating her ass in his face has to be on a mission. Since I was in need of a new identity I decided to keep fucking with Omar, but my instinct said don't mess with the dude.

As I'm sitting in the house waiting for my clothes to dry granny handed me the phone. She said it was my sister calling, but it wasn't. It was Jackie. Granny's Alzheimer's was getting worse by the day, but frankly who cared.

"What?" I answered in an abrupt tone, "no you can't borrow no money no!"

"I ain't askin' you for no fuckin' money. Ever since dat shit came on the news you been actin' real extra Jaz. I called your stinkin' ass cause I had a surprise for you, but fuck it now," Jackie caught an attitude and hung up.

Fuck Jackie she was such a drama queen I took what she said with a grain of salt. I didn't have time to wonder what surprise she had in store for me. My mind was wondering where the hell Omar was because he was late picking me up. He was supposed meet me at my grandmother's crib an hour ago, so we could go meet with the dude with the identity connections.

Just before I got the chance to blow up his phone I heard a knock at the door.

"Where were you man I was getting worried?" I hugged him to see if he was strapped, "We still on?"

"Yeah let me just take a piss first," Omar said, as he adjusted the small pistol in his waist.

Omar must have been heavenly influenced by old blacksplotation flicks growing up, because he had a hooked up Cadillac Seville with Burberry print leather seats, gold spoke rims and furry dice hanging from the rearview. Without explanation I insisted he drive my Benz instead.

During the ride to Jackson Heights, a prevalent Hispanic area in Queens, Omar and I talked about the new club he was telling me about. When he mentioned the name *Candy Bar Lounge* I acted as if I wasn't familiar with the place, but I heard all about it from other dancers. The Candy Bar Lounge was a sleazy hole in the wall located in the hoe headquarters of the eastern seaboard: Hunts Point.

The only kind of girls that worked at the Candy Bar Lounge was underage runaways, ugly worn out street tricks and illegal aliens. It was the kind of place where the patrons didn't care if you had one leg and tits down to your knees, as long as you got them off, they didn't give a shit how old you were or what you looked like.

When we finally got off the sluggish BQE, we pulled up to a Mexican music and video storefront. Inside they sold CD's and DVD's like they advertised, but downstairs they had a graphics art printing shop that appeared to manufacture party flyers and business cards. Now all the way in the back of that place was the real deal operation.

"Was'sup Charlie?" Omar greeted the young looking Mexican girl, "I brought you another customer in need of your services."

All this time I had thought Charlie was a man, but Charlie was a chica. She was a little bit of a thing too. The girl had to be no more than twenty or twenty-two and she stood about five feet tall.

"What can I do for jew today?" Charlie asked.

"I need a good I.D to move across the country without getting knocked," I answered, "I got a thousand on me right now what can we work out? I hear you're the person to make all my dreams come true."

"Maybe I am," Charlie stared deep into my eyes to see if I was a cop, "Maybe I'm not."

Charlie was a wizard with the computer. She somehow logged into the Criminal records database to make sure I was telling the truth about my true identity. Needless to say my name popped up as a wanted felon in Connecticut. Charlie then cut her cigar with a cigar cutter then went on to explain the intricacies of how her business worked.

"Visa's, no problemo. Pes'sports, social security number, birt' certificate, dri'ber license, green card, whatever jew need I can get for jew, but by looking at jour record jew need a body tag to stay out of jail and dat's goin to cost more dan a thousand."

"Body tag? What do you mean I need a body tag?" I asked, truly puzzled, "I just need a I.D."

"Dere was a small town in my country where jung boys and girls turned up missing everyday. Deir bodies were never found and deir families didn't know what happened to dem. As time went on we learned dat Americans who had trouble with de law or worse, de IRS, were crossing da border and kidnapping our people for deir identities to start deir lives over. Like any other Mexican dey would apply for a green card or citizen'chip and actually get approved under the person's name they killed, derefore escaping de law as a naturalized citizen when all along dey were born in de States. Things are a lil' different nowadays," Charlie smiled at me as she puffed rigorously on her cigar, "...a body tag is a term we use in Mexico when someone takes de identity of dead American citizens to sneak into dis land. Jew won't believe the number of college kids dat come into my country to buy prescription drugs. A lot of dem O.D and never make it back across da border. We keep their I.D's and bury da bodies, so unless jew happen to run into Xochiquetzal no one else will know who jew really are except jew and me."

After wondering who the fuck Xochiquetzal was, I handed over the down payment of $1000. Charlie then handed me three New York State Drivers Licenses with her face on each under three different aliases. She asked me to pick which one I thought was authentic, but I couldn't tell. The reason why I couldn't point out the real from the fake was that all of the drivers' licenses were indeed authentic.

Charlie had family members that worked for the Department of Motor Vehicles on her team as well as an aunt in the Social security office. All I had to do was go to the specified DMV where one of Charlie's people would enter my face into the system under an assumed name. After looking over a long list of dead girls on a spiral notebook I chose a pseudonym I thought would fit me best. The person I chose to impersonate was this girl named *Tracy Carbone*, a young Italian girl who Charlie said was last seen in Los Cabos, Mexico with her friends in 1997.

"Can I really open up a bank account under this name?" I questioned with disbelief.

"I no see why not? Jew can even build credit. How jew think terrorist sneak into dis country?"

For a new life $4000 wasn't all that expensive. However I still had to come up with the remaining three K in no less than ten days. Charlie made it clear that she would have me killed if I told anyone about what she does. She also affirmed that if for some reason I were unable to pay in time I would lose the down payment and maybe still lose my life.

Charlie had her shit together I must say. I thanked Omar for hooking me up by giving him a quick hand job in my car before politely asking he get out and go. Following that sticky situation, I drove to a hair supply store in Mt. Vernon where I purchased a blonde wig. I liked how I looked with my hair long, but ever since Chiffon had vindictively cut off my hair I kept it in a crop. Now with some color contacts and a fake Cindy Crawford mole on my cheek, I figured I could throw the police off a little more until it was time to head out west.

If everything went according to plan by the end of the month I would be basking in the California sun doing the damn thing.

Not For Nothing

I had less than two weeks left to get the rest of the money to Charlie and I was beginning to get worried that I wouldn't be able to come through on time. If I had kept my ass at Sue's instead of listening to Omar, I probably would have had the money I needed by now. Dancing at The Candy Bar Lounge was like dancing for free in a regular nightclub. At least in a regular club, guys buy you drinks and if your game is tight you might even get a little paper off them too. With pimp ass Omar taking his cut after every lap dance, I think I was averaging a measly $100 a night compared to the $600 a night I use to earn on a slow night in Sue's.

The customers at Sue's Rendezvous spoiled me and tipped big, but the guys who came into the Candy Bar Lounge were disrespectful and cheap as a Canal

Street Rolex. At this rate there was no way that I was going to make five gees in ten days. Well at least not legally.

In the past most of the money I made dancing went toward my car note, cell phone bill, a steady coke habit and other miscellaneous shit. The only way to make some real money in the Candy Bar Lounge was to trick. And when I say trick, I don't mean giving ordinary blowjobs in the champagne room either. I'm talking about doing some weird shit even the nastiest porn star would be embarrassed to do.

Every business has its niche and the Candy Bar Lounge was no different. On particular nights bands of perverts flocked to the Hunts Point section of the Bronx, where the club was located. Only on those special nights would cars and limos with out-of-state plates pack the curbsides outside the tawdry strip club. I would question what was going on, because oddly enough, with all those cars outside the bar area was empty. I know I seen people walk through the door, but where in the hell did they go I wondered?

That's when I found out later that the Candy Bar Lounge had an upstairs, an exclusively private floor for the hardcore perverts. Unless you were an Asian businessman, or an Internet porn provider or you ran an escort service, the chances of getting through the door were extremely low if you weren't on the guest list.

Selling sex is the world's oldest profession. In Tokyo for example the Japanese had an abhorrent practice of enslaving women to provide sex for soldiers since World War II, and now in the U.S they created a similar system using underage teens. The Candy Bar Lounge was a front for one of the country's largest child pornography rings. They also lead the nation in human trafficking. Foreign teenagers were sold wholesale to fill message parlors and brothels. Most of the girls were imported from Japan and others were runaway teens from who knows where. The older prostitutes, who were not held against their will, were mostly Brazilian or Dominican strippers looking to make a buck.

One night when a fight broke out downstairs, I was able to elude security and get a better look into the things that went on upstairs. As I made my way through the club I stepped over cum puddles and used condoms. The music was playing extra loud and each section of the club had a different fetish being acted out.

I have to admit that at first I was a bit aroused, but the things they were doing to those ten year olds were sick. What I witnessed was hardcore Sado masochistic child molestation. Bats up the ass and tortuous sex machine type shit. I even saw a man with a real whip giving out real ass whippings. I couldn't believe it, in another room they were videotaping old men pissing and shitting on a couple girls, while five more wrinkled fuckers jerked off into one big cup for the girls to supposedly take pleasure in drinking.

What the fuck did I get myself into? The shit going on was outrageous. I was so flustered I had a flashback of my father and puked in a corner. That's when I decided to say screw this place and quit. Omar of course was not happy with my decision to retire my g-string. He claimed if I quit so soon he wouldn't get credit for meeting his stripper delivery quota like I really gave a fuck. Omar thought he was my pimp, just because he got me the job.

While I gathered my costumes and belongings from the locker room Omar encourage me to stay by threatening to turn me into the police. He slapped me around a couple of times then tried talking nicely again.

"That's how it goes in this game baby... you make the money then give it to me you got that baby? I could have been turned you in for the reward money but I like you, so do as I say and you'll be fine."

"First of all I'm not your baby and for someone whose always wearing a 'Stop Snitching' t-shirt you surprise me. I thought you were a G," I mocked as I sipped my Heineken then spit beer in Omar's face.

Omar grabbed me by the tits, which ripped my shirt in the process. As he poked me in the forehead telling me what I was going to do or else, I broke a beer bottle over his head and then jabbed the sharp edge into the side of his neck.

"Get your hands off me you bitch ass snitch! It's hard to talk shit with a piece of glass wedged in your throat huh?"

Omar could only lean against the locker while I retrieved the money he shook me down for. His gun was in the car so there was nothing he could do except bleed. None of the other dancers liked Omar either, so I knew they wouldn't call the police on me. With all the criminal activity going on in the club it would be hours before the bouncers found him, so I left and never looked back.

I had to come up with a new plan and quick. There was one person I had in mind that just might be able to plug me in with the right victims.

"Hey Jackie what's up girl, I just called to see if you wanted to hang out or something. Where you at?"

"Where else? Brooklyn," Jackie sucked her teeth, "why you actin' so nice to me all of a sudden Jaz? What'chu want money!"

"No don't be silly. I thought about it and I was

wrong for blaming you for my problems. I'm a grown ass woman. How do I look being mad at my only true friend in New York City," I buttered Jackie up, "c'mon it's nice outside and I even got a eight ball we could sniff so what's up?"

"Aw'right Jaz but don't be getting' all moody on me and shit. You rememba' how to get to my spot?"

"Yeah I'll be there in about a half," I said as I closed my cell.

After I picked Jackie up we stopped by *Juniors* to get some cheesecake.

"So what was the big surprise you had for me the other day?" I asked Jackie as we sat at the table waiting for the rest of our food, "Cause you know how I feel about surprises," I added, all the while holding my fork under the table just in case her surprise involved a razor.

"It was no biggie. I was just at somebody's crib and I know you were dyin' to see" Jackie acknowledged, while she chewed, "an old friend of yours."

"Who?" I wondered for a second before it hit me, "not Kayla?"

Jackie never said yes, she just nodded her head as she gobbled down her scrumptious cheesecake. I put my fork away for the moment and started eating with ease. Anyhow I still didn't trust the bitch.

"Damn it's been almost six years since I seen Kayla. I wonder if she still has that killer body?"

"All I'm gonna' say is dat she put on a whole lot of weight," Jackie smiled.

"Don't tell me she got all fat and shit," I laughed hoping Kayla was a whale now, "for real Jackie stop playing! Stretch mark fat?" I cackled.

"Why not see for yourself?" Jackie wiped her mouth, "She lives not to far from here, lets stop by for a minute."

Seeing an old acquaintance never really excited me, but this time I couldn't wait to see how ugly and fat Kayla got so I could make fun of her. I know if I fell off or gained eighty pounds she would clown me to no end, so why not do her the same?

As we cruised down Halsey Ave in the Bed-Stuy section of Brooklyn I took in all there was to see. I didn't know that there was so many West Indians living in Brooklyn, until I seen all those island flags.

"Turn here, down Lewis and park by this van."

Instead of walking into the classic looking brownstone Jackie had pointed out, we made our way into a daycare that was connected to the side of the building instead. The sign above our heads read 'Seeds Daycare Center' with red, black and green flags on each side.

"Don't say nothin' about dat shit at the hotel" Jackie smirked, as rambunctious children ran circles around our legs, "cause Kayla and them be on some righteous vigilante shit. They be doin' the same shit we be doin' but they try to convince themselves that their helping out the community."

Off to the side were a group of some more children sitting on the floor Indian style. Kayla was in a rocking chair reading them a story until I interrupted by clearing my throat.

"Jaz? Jasmine O'Reilly?" Kayla screeched, recognizing me right away. "Hole-lee shit it must be the end of the world what the hell is up gurl!"

"You!" I squealed back, as we embraced like old friends do.

"Sup" Kayla unenthusiastically greeted Jackie.

"Look at you and that big belly," I stood back to take a look at Kayla, "you actually look great" I smirked at Jackie for not telling me.

Unfortunately Kayla really did look good I disappointedly admit. She was eight months with that pregnant woman glow. My hopes were Kayla was just plain ole fat so I could gloat.

"And look at you" Kayla paused, "you got so... um big up top damn!"

Even though it had gotten much flatter since the surgery I laughed as I stuck out my butt, "milk does a body good, but I would never expect you to be running a daycare," I changed the subject "you couldn't stand kids!"

"People change and somebody had to step up. If it weren't for us a lot of parents would have to work two jobs just to pay for daycare, so we provide topnotch care at a minimal price... excuse me Gina can you finish reading the children their story, I'm going upstairs to talk with my girl for a minute I appreciate it."

Gina smiled pleasantly as Kayla wobbled with us out the door. At one time Kayla's aunt Gina was strung out on drugs, and even though Kayla wanted to, she never gave up on Gina. Unlike Jackie depicted, it was obvious that Kayla and her crew were really doing positive things in the hood. Besides an occasional spat or two, the Buck fifty Bitches had all matured into loving women with husbands and a home except coke sniffing Jackie.

Jackie was living her life as if she was still in high school. I guess seeing the rest of the click doing things with their lives caused her to be resentful. Personally I thought Jackie was a hater, yet I could still identify with how she felt because in a lot of ways she was just like me. We both could care less about some stupid community programs and we damn sure weren't concerned with helping out the less fortunate. We were both about that cash.

As Kayla fixed herself some Red Raspberry tea, Jackie and I opted for the cold Guinness Stout her husband left in the fridge. I was a little upset that Kayla didn't have anything stronger, but she was never really a drinker anyway. Kayla's place was decorated very afro-centric. It was neat and clean and smelled like burnt sage all throughout the apartment. When Kayla drew the shades the sunlight exposed her book collection and I could tell that she was deep into Black Nationalism from some of the titles.

"I didn't get the chance to tell you this Kayla, but I'm truly sorry about what happened to your parents. I feel like it was my fault for leaving the window unlocked."

"So what brings you to Brooklyn?" Kayla ignored my apology, "I hear you're dancing these days. Mt. Vernon is it?"

I looked at Jackie like *damn you told her all my business didn't you?*

"Actually Kayla I quit. Right now I'm just trying to get myself together ya know."

"You don't have to demean yourself if you don't want to Jaz. How good are you changing diapers?" Kayla asked, "We need all the help we can get around here. I got bills stacked to the knees and not enough help or time."

"Are you offering me a job Kayla?" I replied truly flattered, "Because I would love to work with you."

I had a soft spot for kids ever since I lost the baby, but I didn't want to tell Kayla that I got shot because then I would probably have to go into detail about other things.

"In our place we don't call our seeds kids, we

call them children, because 'kids' as you say are actually baby goats and goats are known to be sacrificial animals. I think enough children from the hood have been sacrificed na'mean Jaz?"

Jackie got tired of Kayla and I reminiscing, so she asked me to take her home.

"We just stopped by to say hi," Jackie cut in, after downing the rest of her Guinness, "I gotta be somewhere soon so I guess we'll see you later."

"Where yall going? To cop some more blow?" Kayla scoffed when she noticed how red Jackie's nostrils were, "Jackie you need to leave that shit alone."

"What I do is my business! I'm baby sitting for your information," Jackie cut her eyes, "c'mon Jaz lets go people got attitudes and shit."

Jackie had some nerve speaking for me, but I happened to be ready to leave anyway so I didn't stress the issue.

"If you're serious about the job Jaz, be here tomorrow morning seven sharp," Kayla reminded while she hugged me goodbye.

During the drive back to Jackie's I learned a lot bout how she felt about her old crew.

"How you gonna' hire crack heads to work for you, but fire me for doin' a couple of lines," Jackie shook her head in revulsion, "Kayla needs to get got," Jackie stated coolly as she did her lipstick in the passenger side mirror, "if you're really as ruthless as you claim you are Jaz I say you roll wit me on this. There's a lot of doe in her crib and I got plans to take it."

Ever since Riva's death, Jackie and Kayla had been at each other's throat. Jackie claimed the reason why they didn't get along anymore was because Kayla never showed up for Riva's funeral, but the real reason why there was so much tension was because of Jackie's growing drug problem. I just let Jackie vent till she was blue in the face.

"Yo she got about half a mill stacked up in dat crib easy! And not for nothin' I don't care how long I knew her ass for half a mill I'll probably rob my own mother," Jackie confessed.

"I think I just found a way to get the six K I need," I thought to myself, "You know where she hides it?" I asked Jackie, while passing her bottle back.

"She keeps it in the basement. In an old water heater we turned into a safe back in da days. You down or what? "

"Yeah I'm wit it. Just let me check something out first," I agreed as I pulled over to let Jackie out, "you heard what Kayla said *without a plan, you plan to fail,"* I laughed as I threw up a black power fist in mockery.

The next morning I met Kayla and the rest of her employees at the daycare on time. While anxious parents dropped off their children on their way to work, I jumped right in and started working my butt off. Those little nigglets were a lot to handle.

The next day around lunchtime, this handsome Mandingo looking dude with dreads walked in. He was Kayla's husband I assumed, because he rubbed and kissed her belly.

"Gal wha' tings a gwan?" Kayla's husband lightheartedly asked, "Me tell ya' nun 'a dis romp round work all day me wan ya' take it easie' gal, let da' youth dem mash up da' place while me fix ya some food."

"This is my friend Jaz," Kayla introduced me, "we went to school together in Connecticut. Don't ask me how she hooked up with Jackie? Jaz this is my husband Sean and his sister Sade. They just got back from Jamaica and I'm glad they left early cause I've been feeling some strong kicks in my stomach."

Kayla's husband seemed nice, but his sister kept looking at me funny. She made me feel out of place.

"Kayla can I speak to you for a minute?" Sade looked all serious, "It's important."

While Kayla and Sade talked in the kitchen, I flirted with Kayla's husband by complementing his wholesome looking dreadlocks. He gave me no play though. I don't think he liked white girls, but oh well he didn't know what he was missing.

"What's so important?" Kayla sat down with Sade's help.

"I think I seen that white girl before," Sade got excited then lowered her voice, "I think I seen her on the news a couple of days before we left."

Kayla doubted Sade's accusation and laughed.

"Yo don't sleep," Sade raised her brow, "it's always the innocent looking ones that turn out to be serial killers and shit. But more importantly she can bring the heat down on us ya feel me?"

Kayla never approached me concerning her conversation with Sade. She let me work all day without mentioning it even once. After Sade left I started to notice Kayla's aunt staring at me funny now too, but I didn't have a clue as to why. At the very end of the day Sade finally confronted me as we stood side by side putting away some toys.

"Yo what you do is your business, but you're gonna' bring the boys down on us and get everybody else popped in the process. The police been watching us for a minute and they might get the wrong idea and think we were in on your little robbery at the Hilton. Yeah that's right I know who you are and I think you should just leave before you get hurt," Sade threatened, as she stood in front of me, "so there's the door. Bye."

Kayla heard us arguing and waddled over to where we were right away. Her big belly kept us apart.

"Whoa whoa wait a minute wait a minute" Kayla stood between us as I reached for my box cutter.

Before I could make up a lie to defend myself against Sade's accusations, here comes Toya with an old copy of the Daily News with my picture in it. Toya handed the paper to Sade who was grilling me the entire time like I was going to slash the side of her face.

"Look I told you!" Sade scowled, "That bitch is probably a crack head just like Jackie."

Kayla smiled as if she was let down, "I owe you an apology Sade and as for you Jaz you need to bounce before it gets really ugly in here. I let you in my house and give you a job and you can't respect me enough to tell me that you're wanted for murder. The police been trying to take us down for years and we can't afford to get affiliated with you. We ain't teenagers no more grow the fuck up."

"But Kayla let me explain..."

"No buts bitch get your ass outta here right now" Sade declared as she reached for her pistol, "and tell Jackie she's not welcomed around here no more either!"

"That ain't necessary," Kayla lowered Sade's hand, "put that shit away before somebody sees you."

As soon as I got in my car I called Jackie.

"Yo you got your thing on you!"

"Of course I got my thing on me why?" Jackie asked excited.

"Your punk ass girl Sade just pulled a gun on me and she said if she ever sees us again, she's gonna' light our shit up. She called you a crack head and told me to tell you don't even think about coming around."

"What! Fuck Sade, fuck all dem conniving bitches! Pick me up when it gets dark I got something for their ass. Tonight we gon' get dat paper!"

My plan was working. The next person I called was Charlie. I wanted to make sure we were still on for tomorrow. Charlie said everything was ready all she was waiting for was the rest of the money.

The window of opportunity was open. When I got back to granny's I started packing for my final east coast departure. All I needed was my toothbrush, a washcloth, two sets of clothes, my wig, my little bit of money and my small photo album. I waited until it got dark like Jackie suggested and while granny watched her T.V programs I tip toed out the door dressed in all black. I would have said goodbye to granny, but she probably wouldn't even remember if I did so or not.

It was a good thing I left the house when I did, because just as I turned the corner I noticed the repo man in my rear view lurking around granny's driveway looking for my Benz. For weeks I had been parking the car in different locations because I stopped paying the car note months ago. It was either pay the car note or pay the coke dealer.

While hitting corners doing 50 mph I thought I was in the clear until a tow truck sped up behind me. When he flashed his high beams I sped off onto the Bronx River Parkway where I lost him for good in mere seconds.

Jackie was waiting for me outside her apartment when I pulled up an hour later than planned. She kept bitching and moaning about my punctuality and

I was not in the mood to put up with her shit.

"Next time I tell you to be here at nine you better be here at nine not ten you stupid ass! Timing is everything! Kayla and her husband pick his mother up from work at ten almost every night. The house is empty for about thirty minutes, which would've been the perfect time to bum rush the spot, get the loot and be out, but no you gotta show up all late and shit," Jackie sucked her teeth in hindsight.

"Just buckle your seat," I said with a scowl.

When we got near Kayla's we noticed Kayla's truck was out front, which could only mean somebody was home.

"I say we just bust in there and shoot everybody's ass. Whatchu' think Jaz?"

"Nah I got a better plan hold on!"

What I did was unexpectedly floor the Benz right into the daycare center window. It was a bad idea because the cars engine caught on fire faster than I thought it would. I was able to escape before it blew, but Jackie couldn't get out in time because I rigged her seatbelt.

"Jaz help me I'm stuck! Help me get out I'm fuckin' stuck!"

Jackie screamed more and more as the flames seethed through the vents.

"Hand me your gun," I demanded, "hand me the gun!"

After Jackie reluctantly handed me her gun, I tossed my cigarette in her lap and ran for the exit.

"See ya later Jackie."

By now the car was engulfed in flames. The moment my feet hit the sidewalk the car exploded and a ball of fire erupted torching everything in its path.

"*One down, two to go,*" I thought to myself.

When people came rushing outside I fell to the ground as if the blast had blown me to the ground. Kayla's husband was one of the first to come to my aid. He picked me up and brought me inside. As soon as he opened the door I shot him under his chin with Jackie's gun.

"Sean!" Kayla screamed out, "Sean answer me! What's going on?"

Sean was dead. Kayla couldn't get out of bed to see for herself, because the explosion and gunshots must have caused her to go into labor. She kept calling out for his help until I walked in the room with Jackie's gun aimed in her direction. Blood speckles covered my pale face.

"Jaz? ... *AW man,*" Kayla held her stomach in pain, "the baby's coming... Sean I need you! SEAN!"

"Sorry, but Sean has left the building. Where's the money?" I asked coldly, "Jackie already told me that you got a stash so don't lie. If you tell me where it is maybe I'll help you. I already checked the basement and there's nothing. So where's the goddamn money Kay?"

"I can't believe you," Kayla continued to moan in pain, "look in that box over there" she struggled to say.

I kept my gun on Kayla while I lifted the lid off the Timberland shoebox. Inside there was about forty five thousand.

"Where's the rest!" I shouted, "I know you got more!"

"Fuck you that'sall of it," Kayla affirmed in agonizing pain, "I told you we got bills... a*w my baby's coming."*

For some reason I believed Kayla was telling me the truth, so I helped her despite all the sirens and flashing lights outside the building. I gathered clean towels and hot water and helped her through the delivery until I heard Sade's voice call up to her.

I hid in the darkness of the unlit hallway. And until the sound of her footsteps climbing the stairs got louder I just fired until I heard Sade's body roll back down.

I couldn't have been as heartless as people said I was, because why would I hang around to help Kayla deliver. Her vagina was dilated and I could see the baby's head. As I rushed to get another clean pot of hot water from the kitchen, Sade shot at me but missed.

"Fuck!" I screamed in surprise.

To my surprise Sade was still alive and had crawled all the way back upstairs into the apartment. I dove on her and we tousled for a minute fighting over the gun. Somehow she managed to slice me with my own box cutter, but as Sade tried to cut me again, I got a hold on her weapon and fired until there were no more bullets left.

I decided it was time to get the fuck out of there, but not before leaving with something even more precious than my freedom.

I ran back into Kayla's bedroom where she was clinched to a bloody baby boy who she practically delivered on her own. Kayla tried to stop me but she was exhausted and weak.

"I'm gonna' see you burn," Kayla muttered.

She couldn't even get up off the bed. I should have finished Kayla off, but I didn't. Instead I just cut the umbilical cord with my razor and left with the baby *and* the money.

I wrapped the infant in layers with a clean towel before throwing a small blanket over him. I knew my face was cut, but it didn't feel like it was that deep. While the firefighters fought with the blaze in Kayla's daycare I disappeared into the subway system a block away.

Even though the train was empty the baby was going ape shit over the screeching sounds of metal against metal. I started to panic. My first thoughts were to just leave the baby on the train and go for self. Then I decided to shut him up by letting him suck on my barren nipple till we got to a stop in Queens. It was about 2 A.M when we arrived in Jackson Heights. The only things open were McDonalds and ironically a Duane Reade where I purchased a few things for my face such as peroxide, gauze and bandages. I also snatched up a baby bottle and some milk the baby could actually drink. Like the many homeless people in New York, I spent the rest of the night in a McDonald's restroom cuddling the child God must have meant me to have.

The next morning I met Charlie at her shop around 10 A.M.

"Jew look like chit," Charlie commented.

"Thank you very much I had a rough night," I bypassed her comment, "here's the rest of what I owe you."

"I didn't know jew had a baby?"

"I didn't know either can we hurry this thing up?"

"Wassup with jew face?" Charlie kept stalling, "jew should have Oscar take a look at that. It's not a good look for jew big picture."

"Don't worry about it, it's a scratch, can I see this for a minute?"

While Charlie counted her cash I hurried through the newspaper on her desk to see if there was any information about last night. There was nothing and I was not about to hang around and wait for a story. For an extra five hundred dollars Charlie quickly produced the baby a birth certificate on her industrial laser printer. After her brother in law sutured my cut, which needed stitches, Charlie gave me a ride to the DMV where her people worked.

"When you get to the front desk ask for Maria," Charlie instructed, as she slid me a manila folder, "hand her this and she'll take it from there."

As usual the DMV was flooded with people out the damn door. For twenty bucks I got this high school kid to hold the baby for me, when it came time for me to take my shitty picture. Being that the stitches followed the contour of my jaw you couldn't tell that I was injured from looking at my I.D. After I kissed my new drivers license I took hold of the baby then walked to the bus stop. Just as Charlie promised everything went smoothly. I was in and out of there in forty-five minutes.

The bus took too long for me, so we caught a cab to LaGuardia airport, where I purchased tickets for the first flight headed for California. As the plane left the ground I smiled uncontrollably singing lullabies to my son. I was officially a new mom with a new outlook on life and as long as the plane didn't crash nothing was going to stop us.

A New Day

At first I blamed myself for everything. Out of frustration and sadness I even tried to kill myself by driving my truck off the FDR drive into the East River. Fortunately someone was watching over me and the car got stuck on a guardrail instead of plunging into the cold murky water. One thing led to another and the next thing I know I was held up in Bellevue Hospital. Doctors diagnosed me as a suicidal-manic-depressive who needed to be monitored for mental observation. Regardless of what they thought, I knew I wasn't that crazy. I was just extremely depressed, miserable beyond belief.

Inside it felt like I was slowly dying. It was impossible not to think about my baby boy or wonder if he was alive or not. All day I would envision those big brown eyes gazing up at mine and more times than

I could count the thoughts of cradling my little angel replayed in my mind over and over again. It was those few seconds of precious memory that got me through the day.

Being locked in an all white room, with white girls who reminded me of Jaz, for twenty-three hours a day didn't help boost my dejected frame of mind either. At night I would stare out of the caged window for hours thinking of all the terrible things I would do to Jasmine if I ever caught up with her wicked ass again. Before long all of my depression turned into hate. I wanted to live now and the only person I wanted to see dead was the bitch who tore my newborn from my hands and shot my husband and friends. Revenge was all worth living for.

One night while I was sleep I heard a child's voice call out to me in a dream. There was no face attached to the sweet calling voice, but I wanted to believe it was my son. He told me to look for him in the sunset. My interpretation of the dream was just; get the fuck out of that insane asylum and search for your son.

If I was not crazy when I first went into Bellevue I sure would be by the time they decided to let me out. What was supposed to remain a thirty-day observation, ended up turning into sixty days, then ninety days of complete redundancy. Since the State of New York pays for the evaluation, the hospital prolongs the process to run up the bill. Basically they were stretching my time for cash, so the next time the frail nurse who gave out the medication opened the door, I knocked her out with a metal tray then stole her keys and escaped. That was the last they ever saw of the girl in room 730.

I called my friend Toya and she quickly came to

my aid. Without even asking Toya provided me with a pistol and some money. Following a warm bath and a hot meal at her apartment in Queens we took a quick trip up to Connecticut to look for some answers. I needed to speak with Jasmine's brother Chad. He was my only hope for some serious clues as to where I could possibly find my son. The interrogation of Chad and his wife led to something worth investigating. Chad said he did not know exactly where his sister was, but he suspected she was in California with his other sister Jenny. I thanked Chad and his wife for all their help by letting them keep their lives.

With the help of the Internet, I easily located the home address Toya forced Chad to write down. I was anxious to head out west. There was no time to wait, but trying to book a flight would have been a stupid thing for me to do considering my popularity with the police. So like back in the days when I would visit my people down in Philly, I opted to take a Greyhound bus across the country.

At Penn Station Toya and I hugged, but we didn't say goodbye to each other because I planned on seeing her again.

"Do what you gotta do and don't forget that you got a place to come back to," Toya encouraged, "by the time you return I'll have the center up and running again."

I could not thank Toya enough. As the departure announcement sounded over the loud speaker I faded into the abyss of travelers with a mission to reclaim my future.

It took almost four days to get to Los Angles and the whole way I just focused my mind on settling the score. For two years and counting Jasmine had evaded the law living the life in California. As far as anyone out west was concerned she was Tracey Carbone, a nice Italian girl from Boston. No one suspected she was a fugitive on the run for murder. Not even her husband or the public school system where she worked as a second grade teacher now.

Even though Jasmine had a new identity, she was still the same trifling skank up to no good. About two months following her appearance in Cali Jasmine's grandmother suffered an unusual fall down a flight of stairs and died. Chad confessed that he thought since Jaz was written out of his grandmothers will for causing the family shame, in addition to Jenny's doctor friend leaving her to go back to his wife, he suspected his sisters plotted to take granny out.

Chad sounded like he was only surmising, but actually his suspicions were right. Jaz did push her grandmother down the stairs for money. Iniquity seems to run in the family. With the old lady dead, Jenny could collect her piece of the pie early, then break Jaz off a share of the 2.5 million dollar inheritance left to her. Well into the bargain for Jaz, Jenny also turned over her beachfront property that she owned to her cruel and twisted sibling for a bigger place in Beverly Hills.

So from the bus station in L.A, I took a cab to the address in Santa Monica. Every home in Santa Monica was in picture perfect condition. Talk about quiet, every street was a gated community, but nobody seemed to mind the black girl in fatigues walking through their lawns to get to the beach. The sound of waves crashing against the rocks held my attention for a minute until this lady walking her dog stopped to talk.

"Hi there, are ya thinking about buying Brian and Tracey's place?" She asked, as I matched the address to the paper that I held in front of my face.

"Maybe?" I answered as friendly as I could, before bending down to rub her dog's head, "If the price is right I will. Do you think they'll mind if I peek inside to get a better look at the place?"

"No way. Go right ahead... Sparky must like you. He never acts this way around strangers... anyway hope you like what you see. This is a nice area and you look like a nice person... what did you say your name was again?"

The goofy acting lady was getting a little too nosey for me so I cut the conversation short and walked around the back. Behind the row of condos revealed a long stretch of beautiful white sand and a slew of yachts floating out to sea. I took my time to take in the picturesque view of the ocean then pumped myself to break into the house like I planned.

Growing up in the projects I had acquired a few locksmith skills and used them to get into the backdoor. I could have just kicked in the damn door since nobody was around and no alarm was visible, but why risk it? Like a bounty hunter in pursuit of a fugitive, I carefully entered with my gun aimed in front of me ready to shoot. The first floor was clear, but as I stumbled upon a room upstairs I let down my guard. My heart beat faster than a drum machine as I looked over all the toys and stuffed animals. I ran to the closet where there was a closet full of baby clothes.

Quickly I inspected the labels for gender and size. To my elation most of the tags read 2T, which was the exact size a two year old would wear. A smile of slight satisfaction emerged on my face, as faith crept over the bleak horizon of doubt I carried with me for two years.

"He's alive I know it. This has to be his room" I

contemplated, "*I know my son is here these have to be his clothes*," I was certain, hugging and smelling the Oshkosh jumper as if my precious was still in it.

More tears streamed down my cheek as a picture in the hallway caught my eye. I finally let go of the baby clothes I clung to and walked toward the framed 8 x 10 hanging on the wall. What I was staring at was a spitting image of my husband, only two years old. My baby was a little cutie pie. Seeing that face was sweetest thing I had ever saw. I could not stop crying I was so happy. I placed my gun on stand and examined the picture more closely.

In the middle of my euphoria the phone rang and I ran back downstairs with my piece in hand. By the time I found the phone the machine came on.

"Hey guys it's Pete, I just called to let you know that I found a buyer for your place and they're ready to close as soon as you are. Give me a call tomorrow or whenever you get back from your honeymoon...have a good one adios."

Jasmine and her husband were in Jamaica on their honeymoon. I knew my son was with someone else and not in Jamaica with the newlyweds, because there was a note on the refrigerator with instructions of when to give 'Duane' his cough medicine. I couldn't believe that piece of shit named my son after one of her drug-dealing boyfriends from the past.

By nightfall I had inspected every nook and cranny as good as any crime scene investigator. I carefully scoured the condo instead of ransacking the place because I wanted to maintain the element of surprise when they walked in and found me sitting on their couch. However soon after fixing myself something to eat I heard a key at the door. I grabbed my gun and hid in the kitchen. As the crumpling bag sound got closer I prepared myself. Before she could place the bags of groceries on the granite countertop I pistol-whipped the woman from behind.

Sorry to say it wasn't Jaz or her sister on the floor. The woman that I knocked out was some middle aged Spanish woman. When I turned around to see if she was alone, the boy from the picture was staring at me with a puzzled look on his adorable little face.

"Oh my God!" I picked him up and spun him around, "my baby, my baby boy, my handsome baby boy!"

I kissed him all over, but I must've hugged my boy too tight or I frightened him with my high-pitched excitement. He started crying to no end.

"I know, I know, I scared you didn't I? I'm sorry, come here, lets gets you some cookies... my name is Kayla would you like some cookies?"

I dug into the box of animal crackers I had been munching on while going through the photo album before sitting down on the couch to talk to my son. I acknowledged him as Duane so not to confuse him, but my son was going to be named after his father, not some jungle fever having dope pusher.

"I'll be right back Duane," I said in a playful voice, before I looked for something to tie the nanny up with.

The only thing I could come up with as a restraint was the electrical cord from the toaster. I tied her arms behind her back and used the blender cord to bind her legs.

After some more snacks and a cup of juice Duane didn't seem to mind me in the house. He forgot all about Elke and we sat on the couch watching Nickelodeon until she came to. I did all the talking and found out that my son liked to watch Thomas the

Tank Engine. He said it was his favorite.

When Elke regained coconsciousness I made clear that I was not going to hurt her as long as she cooperated and listened to me. I tried to explain to her that the boy she took care of six days out of seven was actually my son. To prove to her that Jaz was never in the Peace Corps and did not adopt Duane from some African village like she led everyone to believe, I pulled out a picture of my husband and some news clippings that proved Tracey Carbone was in fact Jasmine O'Reilly.

Elke's English was limited, so she had a hard time understanding the details. She begged for me to untie her and suggested I call the police if what I was saying was true. Elke was starting to piss me off, but I had to keep my cool because my son was watching.

"Look! Doesn't Duane look just like the man in this picture?" I asked rhetorically, "Your boss killed him and stole Duane from me right after I delivered him in New York. I've been looking for my baby for over two years and there is no way I'm going to let you, the police or anybody else take him away from me again! STAY QUIET or I'm not going to be so nice!"

According to Elke her boss would be returning home in the morning, however around 2 A.M a car pulled up in the driveway and the bright shine of headlights peaked through the blinds. I had untied Elke and made her identify whose car it was pulling onto the property. After she confirmed it was indeed Jasmine and Brian I sat her back down on the sofa. Duane was asleep in his bed and I wanted to keep it that way. Who knows what damage it would do seeing me kill someone he thinks is his mother.

Jaz and her husband Brian were now in the garage, while I sat on the couch with my gun pointed

Elke in case she decided to act up again.

"Behold... the pale whore has returned," I calmly greeted the both of them as they stepped over the threshold, "drop the luggage and put your hands where I could see'um! Both of you, do it now!"

Jaz's mouth hung wide open and she dropped her strawberry milkshake all over the floor. Her skirt was ruined. When she realized who I was a stream of urine ran down the inside of her leg.

"Here take it," Brian tossed me his wallet, as if I was some petty thief or something, "I have about a hundred dollars in there and you can take anything else that you want too, just don't shoot us! We just got back from our honeymoon please!"

"That rehabilitated hoe standing next to you is not who you think she is," I stated as I threw the newspaper clippings at Brian's feet, "her real name before she married you is Jasmine O'Reilly, AKA fuck face, a piece of shit white trash kidnapper from Fairfield, Connecticut where she's wanted for numerous murders by the way... the bitch stole my son from me only minutes out of my womb. I almost died of depression thinking about my newborn in her arms every night. Can you imagine what's that like?"

"Honey don't believe her," Jaz interrupted, "she's crazy don't believe a word she says!"

"I like what Jenny did to the place, but too bad about your grandmother's nasty fall. Chad sends his love."

Brian looked at his wife then looked at the FBI's most wanted picture I threw at him and started shaking his head in revulsion. He stared at Jaz with a crushed look utterly confused.

"I can't believe this Tracey or Jasmine or whatever your name is? I loved you how could you keep this from me?"

Like the dedicated fool she was Elke jumped on my back kicking and punching. She tried to be a hero I guess. Jaz took off running upstairs while Elke and I struggled. Brian got a hold of my gun and told Elke to call the police while he kept the gun on me.

In an odd case of events Jaz came down the stairs with a snub nose revolver held to Duane's head.

"That won't be necessary Elke" Jaz stopped her dumb ass house slave, "move away from the phone and sit next to Kayla... sientate ahora!"

"Where'd you get that gun?" Brian yelled, "Call the police Elke... don't listen to her can't you see she is just as crazy as this woman?"

Sweat was pouring off of Jaz and she was shaking like a leaf. I tried to comfort Duane with words, but his pretended mommy was scaring him worse than I did.

"When Duane looked at me I always felt like he was staring at me with your eyes Kayla" Jasmine confessed, "I never killed no kid before but I guess I have to now!"

"It doesn't have to be like this" Brian kept repeating, "just give me the gun and we can work this out."

"Why don't you drop *your* gun!" Jaz scowled at Brian, "or I'll shoot this little nigglet I swear!"

"I tried to tell you that your wife's a phony," I admonished before Brian was to slide Jaz my weapon, "she killed her own grandmother and burned her own father alive and killed about nine other people. Do you think she really cares about you? You're nothing to her. If you drop that gun I guarantee you she will shoot all of us and move on to the next location like we never existed. Everything about her is fake especially her love for you! The bitch you married got fake lips, fake booty and fake breasts and you're her fake ass husband with a fake son... *Duane is my flesh and blood whether you like it or not Jaz and no matter what you do you will never be his mother!*"

The more I revealed her past the more Jaz seemed to get agitated, so I kept on talking shit. Brian eventually turned my gun on Jaz, and when he did Elke ran for the front door. In fear that she might call the police Jaz dropped Duane and fired two shots into Elke's back. Brian dove on Jaz struggling to get the revolver from her hand.

Next thing I knew a shot went off and Brian fell to the floor dead. I elbowed Jaz in the throat before I grabbed Duane then tossed him on the side of the couch. As Jasmine stood up to shoot me in the back like she did Elke, I spun around like a ballerina, slashing her face with the box cutter I had between my fingers. I sliced Jaz's forehead in the same motion one would throw a frisbee then I lunged for my gun, which was four feet away.

When I turned around to shoot Jaz was gone. However she left a trail of blood up the stairs this time. As I crept into the second level hallway three shots tore through the wood railing that made up the stairs. Jaz missed me. A snub nose revolver only has six shots, so I knew she was out of ammo, but I didn't know if she reloaded or not. I took a chance and charged in.

"Did you actually think you could get away with this shit Jaz?" I yelled out as I searched each room, "Come out come out wherever you are? I know you're out of ammo Jasmine aren't you?"

The closer my steps got the more I could hear Jaz's heavy breathing. Stupid was trying to hide around the bathroom corner, only her big fake tits poked out past the wall. After I emptied my clip into the sheet rock Jaz fell from behind her hiding place. Both of her kneecaps were blown off and she was bleeding from her side too. It was weird seeing those bloody saline bags ooze out of her chest like that.

In the travails of all of this I found solace in my heart while standing over Jaz. As far as any remorse coming out of her there was none.

"Fuck you Kayla!" Jaz coughed blood.

I spit in her eye as she panted for dear life, and left her with these four simple words: Fuck you too bitch!

Disinclined to kill any longer, I walked away. I'd rather let Jaz choke on her own blood than give her the satisfaction of easing her pain. Biggie Smalls once said 'you're nobody till somebody kills you' and Jaz was definitely a nobody to me. So instead of doing all the terrible things I had dreamt of doing to Jaz, I let time finish her off.

I was a mommy again and there was a little two-year-old boy downstairs that needed me. Duane was more important than watching Jaz die. I got what I wanted. My reprisal was getting my son back.

When I tossed my gun on her lap Jaz thought I was giving her a way out, but I wasn't. I just smiled as the gun clicked and clicked with no boom at the end. She looked so miserable holding that empty pistol to her head hoping to end her own life. I think not. Jaz would die a slow death. She felt exactly how I wanted her to feel. Hopeless.

As I walked out the door with Duane in my arms we both looked toward the sunrise. It was a new day and just like the horizon in all its splendor and beauty I had a sun of my own to raise.

ORDER FORM
address to:
KingPen Ink P.O. Box 6411 Bridgeport, CT 06606

www.TheKingPen.com

Name:____

Inmate #:______________________________________
(necessary for all institution orders)

Address:_______________________________________

____

City:____________________ State:______ Zip:________

BUCK FIFTY $13.00
QTY:_____

PAROLE VIOLATORS $13.00
QTY:______

Shipping/handling $2.00 each book
add $1.00 for each additional book over two

ACCEPTED FORMS OF PAYMENT INCLUDE:

INSTITUTIONAL CHECKS & MONEY ORDERS ONLY

PERSONAL CHECKS WILL NOT BE ACCEPTED AT ALL

Total cost for one book = $15.00

Total cost for two books = $30.00

Amount enclosed $________

KingPen Ink is not responsible for orders denied or withheld by the institution for any reason nor are we responsible if an inmate is relocated within or without the facility

THANK YOU
ONE LOVE

ORDER FORM
address to:
KingPen Ink P.O. Box 6411 Bridgeport, CT 06606

www.TheKingPen.com

Name:______________________________

Inmate #:______________________________
(necessary for all institution orders)

Address:______________________________

____

City:______________ State:______ Zip:______

BUCK FIFTY $13.00
QTY:_____

PAROLE VIOLATORS $13.00
QTY:_____

Shipping/handling $2.00 each book
add $1.00 for each additional book over two

ACCEPTED FORMS OF PAYMENT INCLUDE:

INSTITUTIONAL CHECKS & MONEY ORDERS ONLY

PERSONAL CHECKS WILL NOT BE ACCEPTED AT ALL

Total cost for one book = $15.00

Total cost for two books = $30.00

Amount enclosed $________

KingPen Ink is not responsible for orders denied or withheld by the institution for any reason nor are we responsible if an inmate is relocated within or without the facility

THANK YOU
ONE LOVE

ORDER FORM
address to:
KingPen Ink P.O. Box 6411 Bridgeport, CT 06606

www.TheKingPen.com

Name:________________________________

Inmate #:________________________________
(necessary for all institution orders)

Address:________________________________

____

City:______________ State:________ Zip:________

BUCK FIFTY $13.00
QTY:______

PAROLE VIOLATORS $13.00
QTY:______

Shipping/handling $2.00 each book
add $1.00 for each additional book over two

ACCEPTED FORMS OF PAYMENT INCLUDE:

INSTITUTIONAL CHECKS & MONEY ORDERS ONLY

PERSONAL CHECKS WILL NOT BE ACCEPTED AT ALL

Total cost for one book = $15.00

Total cost for two books = $30.00

Amount enclosed $________

KingPen Ink is not responsible for orders denied or withheld by the institution for any reason nor are we responsible if an inmate is relocated within or without the facility

THANK YOU
ONE LOVE